Spring Break at the Lake House

Annette Vetter Adventure #7

April 1969

by Ann Carol Ulrich

Spring Break at the Lake House

Ann Carol Ulrich

Earth Star Publications
P.O. Box 1213
Cedaredge, CO 81413

FIRST EDITION
First Printing June 2017

ISBN 978-0-944851-49-4

Printed in the United States of America

Cover photo by John Wanserski
www.mywisconsinspace.com

Earth Spaces
http://youtube.com/earthspaces

Earth Spaces Photographs
http://fineartamerica.com/profiles/john-wanserski.html

Other Annette Vetter Books

The Mystery at Hickory Hill
Annette Vetter Adventure #1

The Secret of the Green Paint
Annette Vetter Adventure #2

The Pouting Pumpkin Mystery
Annette Vetter Adventure #3

The Legend of the Lantern
Annette Vetter Adventure #4

In the Shadow of the Tower
Annette Vetter Adventure #5

The Ground Hog Mystery
Annette Vetter Adventure #6

Other Young Adult Books
By Ann Carol Ulrich

The Root Cellar Mystery

Contents

Spring Break
at the
Lake House

ACU

To Vorian, who loves the water

1

An April Morning

"Oh, Mom! Can't they get someone else?" Seated at the breakfast table with her plate of scrambled eggs and a blueberry muffin, Annette reached for the butter dish.

Helen Vetter, dressed in her bathrobe, sat with her cup of coffee and let out a sigh. "I really have to fill in for the nurses who deserve some vacation time," she lamented.

Terry, who had just finished eating his breakfast, pushed his chair back at the kitchen table and stood up to carry his dishes to the sink. "Mom, it was *your* idea going to the lake."

Annette, perturbed, stared into her glass of orange juice. "We were actually supposed to go see Aunt Marie and Uncle Joe at Christmas," she reminded her mother. "But you had to work then, too, I remember."

Ruby emerged from the stairway in the dining room, dressed in a white skirt and scoop-necked aqua sweater with short sleeves. Her blond hair had been brushed back into a ponytail with a matching aqua ribbon. She smiled and said, "Good morning."

"Good morning, Ruby," said Mrs. Vetter. "You look very pretty in that outfit."

"Thank you." Ruby walked to the stove to dish up her

plate and glanced at Annette. "Why are you pouting, Annette?"

Terry, 17, carefully dumped his dirty dishes into the sink. "Mom's not going to the lake house," he told his little sister.

Thirteen-year-old Ruby's blue eyes widened in disbelief as she faced Mrs. Vetter. "Oh, no! We're not going?"

"Of course you're going," Mrs. Vetter reassured her. She took a sip of her coffee. "You and Annette can still go to the Parkers', and Penny too."

"Terry's not going either?" Ruby glanced at her tall blond brother.

"I have to stay and work," he said with an apologetic smile. "I have two jobs now, what with helping Tim and his father at the Duncan farm, and now mending fence at the Randts'."

Annette picked up her fork and let out a big sigh. "I was hoping we could all go as a family," she said as she stabbed at her egg.

"Someone needs to stay home and take care of the live-stock," Terry reminded her.

"Just the cow," said Annette.

"Don't forget the dog and cat," he added, wiping his hands with a kitchen towel.

Ruby brought her plate over to the table and sat next to Annette. "That reminds me ... Mr. Brown said he's getting in an order of baby chicks at his store in a couple of weeks."

"That's good news," said Mrs. Vetter with a smile.

"I'm still sad about the chickens." Ruby hung her head.

Annette reached over and patted her little sister on the shoulder. "We'll start over with a fresh flock of birds," she said. In March, a fox had invaded the chicken house one night and killed all of the birds. Ruby had been devastated. She had taken on the chore of feeding the chickens, cleaning the coop and collecting the eggs and was turning into quite the little poultry farmer. Having been through it a couple of times herself, Annette knew how Ruby felt now, and yet having fresh stock now and then was probably a good thing.

"Anyway," said Mrs. Vetter, cupping her hands around her coffee mug, "I thought that tomorrow morning, we'd all drive up to Minocqua and spend the night at the lake house, and then on Sunday Terry and I can drive back home. At least we can have a family gathering for one night. How does that sound?"

"Groovy!" Ruby perked up immediately and dove into her eggs with her fork.

"Yeah, I'm quite sure I can get the day off tomorrow," said Terry. "Mr. Randt wants me to finish the fence before we have to go back to school after the break. I'm sure I can do it."

"Maybe Tim can take care of the cows," said Annette, "and then you and Mom will be back Sunday night."

"Then it's settled." Mrs. Vetter smiled.

Annette bit into her toast. She would have preferred to have her mother take a week's vacation in Minocqua with them, but when she had changed her work schedule to part-time — after taking in Ruby and Terry — the agreement had been that she'd be available to fill in for vacations at the hospital.

"What kind of chickens are you gonna get?" Terry asked as he put away the pitcher of fresh cow's milk in the refrigerator.

"Kay Randt says Orpingtons would be good," said Ruby. "I kind of want a mixture of them."

A half-grown tabby cat suddenly appeared outside at the kitchen window. It meowed at them and Terry said, "Clyde wants her breakfast."

"Clyde!" Ruby got up and ran to the back door. A moment later, the teen-aged gray kitten strolled in and made her way to her feed dish in the corner by the coat rack. Annette's collie, Ginger, who had been resting at her feet underneath the kitchen table, got up and went to greet his feline friend, his tail swishing gently.

"And if you get a rooster, you'll have your own baby chicks." Annette grinned as Ruby sat back down.

"Can I get a dozen chicks?" Ruby asked their mother.

"Yes, I think a dozen is a good number," agreed Mrs. Vetter and drank more of her coffee.

"How many eggs will a dozen hens lay?" asked Terry.

"Each hen lays one egg a day, as a rule," said Annette. She finished her breakfast, then cleared her place.

Terry did the math in his head. "That means … wow, you'll have a dozen eggs a day."

"Seven dozen in a week," chimed in Ruby with a smile.

"That's a lot of eggs to eat," mumbled Terry.

"We can sell some of them," Annette suggested.

"Really?" Ruby brightened.

Mrs. Vetter nodded. "You might make a small profit after we pay for their feed."

"Oh yeah …" Ruby took a drink of milk.

Annette glanced at the clock, then ran upstairs to get ready for school. Because it was Good Friday, they only had half a day of classes. She was looking forward to spending the next week up in Minocqua. Even though she had envisioned her entire family staying at the lake house with Uncle Joe and Aunt Marie and their daughter, Fern, Annette hoped it would still be fun.

Penny came by promptly at her usual time. Annette — dressed in a lavender empire dress with three-quarter length sleeves and a square neck — grabbed her jacket and headed out the door with Terry, who had changed from his green winter coat to a lighter jacket. Ruby was still eating and Mrs. Vetter stood at the sink, washing the breakfast dishes. Ruby's bus came later to take her to the junior high.

"What a gorgeous day it turned out to be," said Penny on the back porch as they came out to join her in their walk to the bus stop. Penny had on a short beige skirt and white boots. Her long dark hair was pulled back into a ponytail and she sighed with pleasure as her green eyes took in the blue sky and surrounding woods that were just starting to bud out after the long, cold winter.

"I thought spring would never come," said Annette as they walked down the Vetters' driveway.

"And spring break begins today, after school lets out," Terry reminded them, as if they needed to be reminded.

"It's also Good Friday," said Penny. "Annette, I'm so excited about going to Minocqua! Did your mom say when we're leaving?"

Annette quickly explained the change in plans, how Mrs. Vetter had decided to fill in for some other nurses at the hospital and wouldn't be staying up at the lake with them. "But she and Terry are going to drive us up north tomorrow morning. They'll stay the night, then drive back on Sunday."

"Oh, that's a shame," said Penny. "And Terry's not going to stay with us either?"

"No, your dad needs me," said Terry, "Plus I agreed to help the Randts out with their fences."

"Oh, that's right." Penny grinned. "Pete said he had to mend fence during spring break."

Annette stopped at the end of the driveway and pulled an envelope out of her purse to stick in the mailbox.

"Been writing letters again, Annette?" asked Penny.

"Yup. I finally answered Mandy's letter." Annette stuffed the envelope addressed to Gunnison, Colorado, into the box, then shut the door. "Mandy wants to come visit us this summer."

"Cool," said Penny. "That trip we took to Colorado last August was unforgettable."

Terry, who had lived several years in Colorado Springs, smiled as they walked on down the road toward Tower Drive. "I don't miss it that much," he disclosed.

The girls stared at him. "You mean, you like Wisconsin better?" asked Annette.

"Well, let's put it this way," said Terry. "Ravensville is a lot less hectic than living in the big city."

"Sounds like your brother is a small-town kind of guy," Penny said with a laugh.

"Well, Mandy certainly doesn't live in a city," said Annette, remembering the Cochetopa Hills and the Mitchell ranch that she and Penny had visited last summer.

"Don't you miss your friends?" Annette asked her brother as they walked.

He shrugged. "Oh, I suppose … a little. But now I've found my family … my roots … and I really dig it here."

Annette was pleased to hear him say it. She knew that her life had certainly changed for the better when her half-brother had found her and revealed who he was at Christmastime. Her mother being able to accept Terry and his sister, Ruby, into their little family had been the best thing that had ever happened in her life. It had been a dream come true.

"So tell me more about your cousin," Penny prodded, smiling at Annette. "What is Fern like?"

Annette shifted her books and purse to her other side. "It's been a while since I've seen my relatives in Minocqua," she said. "Fern's 17. Aunt Marie is my mom's sister, and Uncle Joe is an ex-Marine."

"He is?" Terry's eyebrows lifted.

"Yes," said Annette. "He enlisted during World War II."

"Gosh," said Terry. "Was he career military?"

"No, I don't think so," said Annette. "Uncle Joe and Aunt Marie run a resort up on Lake Minocqua. They've had it for years, and the lake house is kind of a lodge, where they live year round, but take in guests during the tourist season."

"You've stayed at the lake house before?" asked Terry.

"Oh, sure," said Annette, "not since I was Ruby's age,

though. I have another cousin … David. He's Fern's older brother. He's in the Marines now and I think he's still over in Vietnam."

Terry was silent as they walked. Annette knew her brother was probably thinking about his stepdad, who was Missing in Action over in Vietnam, and was presumed dead.

"Let's not talk about Vietnam," suggested Penny. "It's way too pretty a day to be thinking of that horrible place."

"Ruby's getting baby chicks," said Annette to quickly change the subject. They discussed safer topics as they walked the rest of the way to the bus stop, where several rural kids were waiting. Then, within minutes, the school bus drove up and they boarded.

Penny led Terry and Annette to the rear of the bus, where Pete Randt sat. Annette and Terry took the empty seat in front of him, and Penny joined Pete in his seat.

"Hey, I heard you're gonna take Band next year," Pete said to Penny.

Annette turned in her seat and faced them. "Pen, is that right?"

"Yeah," said Penny. "My piano teacher said I should be taking Band or Orchestra."

"What instrument are you gonna play?" Terry asked.

"Piano's her instrument," said Pete, "but she's gonna be in percussion."

"Drums?" Annette scrunched up her face. "Isn't that what Tim plays?"

"Well, yeah." Penny blushed. "But Mrs. Frye said they'll probably use me on piano, as well as cymbals, bells … and other stuff."

"She'll probably be in the jazz band for sure," said Pete. He turned to her with a smile. "I wouldn't have gotten a First if Penny hadn't accompanied me during Solos & Ensembles this winter."

Penny rolled her eyes and turned away, embarrassed. "It had nothing to do with me."

"It had everything to do with you," insisted Pete. "You're a terrific accompanyer... accomp-pianist ... *aw*, whatever it is you're called."

"Piano player will do," said Penny. "But that's all I did ... *you* practiced hard to earn that First, Pete. I'm proud of you."

"Are *you* taking any electives next year?" Pete asked Annette.

Surprised that the conversation had turned to her, Annette blinked. "Nothing as exciting as Band," she replied. "Probably typing ... and some art. Mom thinks I should take more science."

"Any ideas about where you're headed?" Terry asked Annette.

"What do you mean?"

"You know ... what you wanna do after high school."

"Uh ... not really," Annette admitted.

"What about you, Terry?" Penny asked. "You're gonna be a senior next year."

"Yeah, do you think you'll be headed for college?" asked Pete.

Terry scratched his head. "Gosh ... maybe."

"Terry's real smart," Annette bragged. "Unlike me!"

Penny giggled.

"Now that's not fair," said Pete. "Annette, I think you should go to investigative school and become a detective."

Annette made a face and giggled.

"No, it's true," said Penny, her green eyes widening. "Annette, I'll bet Detective Brennan at the Ravensville Police Department would help you get into the police academy."

"Me?" Annette looked around and noticed some other kids on the bus were staring at her. She lowered her voice. "That's ridiculous."

"No, it isn't," said Terry. "There are lots of women cops."

"And detectives," added Penny. "You have talent when it comes to solving mysteries."

Annette sat back and rode in silence as the conversation drifted in another direction. The reminder of life after high school brought up her feelings of insecurity where Tim Duncan was concerned. Since Tim had become her boyfriend on Valentines Day, they had been seeing more of each other, mostly at the Duncans' house playing pool, going for walks in the woods, or an occasional visit to the drive-in. But Annette knew that Tim would be leaving for college in less than six months now, and she worried about their budding relationship coming to an end.

2

The Acceptance Letter

Home. He wasn't sure where that was anymore. It certainly hadn't been where he remembered it to be.

Just a week ago, Major Bob Foley had been released after his lengthy debriefing. No hero's welcome, no parades … just plenty of paper work, interrogation and physical therapy at Walter Reed Hospital.

He wasn't even sure how long they had kept him there. It could have been a couple of weeks, or a couple of months … there was no telling how long. His memory was a far cry from what it used to be.

On this Friday morning in early April, Bob cruised east on Interstate 70, in a junky rust bucket he'd bought for seventy dollars at a shady used car dealer outside Colorado Springs. The car had a few problems, for sure. It had stained seats, scratches on the paint, a heater that didn't work and the window on the passenger side wouldn't roll down. But the tires were adequate and so far the vehicle seemed to function okay. He hoped it would last till he reached Wisconsin.

Bob considered himself lucky that he could still drive. His left shoulder had been damaged to the point where he would never regain full function of it, but he could steer, at least. His left foot was permanently crippled, which gave him a limp when he walked. But he could reach both the brake and the accelerator with his right foot. The car had no clutch, so that wasn't an issue.

Traffic was sure to pick up by afternoon. Bob knew that this was Easter weekend and that folks would be traveling on the highways. He had little money to his name, so he planned on sleeping at rest areas in his car. A sleeping bag and pillow were on the back seat, along with a heavy coat and a change of clothes which they'd given him before he checked out of the hospital.

With any luck, he'd reach Madison by the next morning and perhaps he'd find Ruby and Terry at their uncle's place. It had been a blow finding out about Ruth. He found out later that officials had tried to contact his wife in Colorado Springs as soon as he had been rescued by the U.S. Navy on the Vietnamese coastline.

Half dead and with no memory of his identity, Major Foley had been treated aboard ship for dysentery and his other unhealed wounds, including two broken arms and his foot injury. Ruth's death had been purposely kept from him until the day of his release from Walter Reed. The Air Force had no knowledge of where his kids were.

"But I'm going to find them," Bob mumbled to himself as he stared ahead at the flat lands of eastern Colorado, headed into Kansas. "We'll be a family again." He had remembered that his wife's brother, Will Knutson, was the only living relative.

One of the neighbors where his wife and kids had lived while he was overseas, fighting the war, had mentioned that they thought the uncle had taken in the kids. It was hard to believe, since Will was somewhat of a recluse.

But it was worth checking out, for sure. Bob hoped he could remember enough to find Will's house in Madison.

Annette had just stepped out the classroom door after her second hour art class. Kids were flooding the halls for the ten-minute break. She was heading toward the sophomore lockers when she heard a familiar voice call out, "Annette!" Turning, she smiled as she saw Tim Duncan, dressed in a dark green turtleneck shirt, headed toward her, his books in one arm.

"Hi, Tim." She waited for him to catch up and they walked together down the hall.

"Hey, I wanted to show you something," he said and steered her over against the lockers while kids passed by them. He reached into one of his books and brought out an envelope, which he gave her.

"What is it?" Annette shifted her books and took the envelope, then read that it was addressed to Timothy Duncan, Route 1, Ogden Road. In the upper left hand corner was the logo for Wisconsin State University—Eau Claire.

"It's my acceptance letter," Tim said with a grin. "I got in."

Annette smiled up at him and was happy for him, yet the old nagging swelled within. "Tim, I'm so glad."

"I knew you'd be as excited as I am," he said and gave her arm an affectionate pinch.

"I'll bet your parents are proud of you," said Annette.

"Yeah, but Dad realizes he's gonna lose his right-hand man when I go off to college in September."

"Well, Terry is probably willing to help him out," she said. "He's already working for your dad part-time, and Terry's a quick learner."

"For a year maybe," said Tim. He tucked the envelope back into his book and they started walking again toward the sophomore lockers. "Then Terry's gonna wanna leave for college."

Annette sighed. "Gee, where does that leave me?" she teased. "As soon as I get a brother, he's getting ready to go off to college … and as soon as I get a boyfriend …"

Tim put his arm around her back and leaned forward. "Hey, let's not think about that right now, okay? Let's just concentrate on what we've got going now."

Annette didn't want Tim to know she was feeling insecure. No promises had been made, and she knew a lot could change in the months ahead. She had no reason to believe that just because she and Tim Duncan were now going steady, there would be a future ahead for them. He was right … it did no good to worry about what lay ahead. All that was important were the days ahead and the summer, before he left home.

"There they are," Penny called ahead of them. She and Pete Randt stood at the locker Annette shared with her best friend. "Guess what? Pete's getting his learner's permit this week."

"Really? That's great news." Annette smiled at Pete, who blushed.

"I'm finally gonna turn fifteen-and-a-half like the rest of you," he said.

"Tim hasn't taken me out for a driving lesson in over a week," Penny complained.

"I've been too busy," he retorted.

"Well, I haven't gone out either," complained Annette. "And Terry's still too young to teach me, even though he turned seventeen last month," she added.

"My dad's gonna take me out on the road," said Pete.

"Annette's doing fairly well with her driving," commented Tim.

"Just think, I'll be sixteen in five weeks," announced Penny, then frowned when she saw Pete's face fall. "Oh, Pete, I'm sorry … but there's no shame in dating an older woman."

Annette and Tim both laughed, and finally Pete managed a smile. "Well, I'd better get to my locker. Third hour is gonna start and I have to turn in a paper."

"See you on the bus," Penny called after him. She turned to Annette. "Are you riding home with Tim today?"

Annette looked up at the dark-haired boy with his attractive green eyes. He smiled down at her and nodded. "Yes," she told her friend.

"Groovy. I'll call you later then."

"Where are you going?" asked Annette. "The bell's not gonna ring for another five minutes."

Penny reached into the locker and pulled out her purse and a book. "I have to go talk to the orchestra teacher about next year," she explained. "I was in seeing Mr. Edwards earlier, and he said I might be able to get an independent study in music."

"What's that?" asked Annette. Mr. Edwards was the assistant principal and a guidance counselor of sorts.

"It means I'd get to be in a class by myself next year, and work on my piano playing ... at school! And I'd get credit for it."

"Well, that's cool ..." Tim looked around. "I guess I'd better find Terry. I wanted to ask him something." He turned to Annette. "See you after fourth hour."

"Okay ... in the parking lot," said Annette. Tim walked away and she turned to her best friend. "Pen, that would be tremendous! You have gotten so good at playing. But I thought you were going to take Band next year."

Penny's green eyes lowered and she tried to hide a smile. "This will be better. To tell you the truth, I felt kind of silly wanting to be in Band and having to learn a different instrument. But I like playing accompaniments for the Band kids. I wish I'd helped out last year."

"Good luck," said Annette.

"I'll talk to you later this afternoon about the trip," said Penny as she started down the hallway. "I'm so excited! Aren't you? I can't wait to see the lake house ..."

Annette stood at her locker and decided to rearrange the mess Penny had left. She knelt down and started pulling out papers, notebooks and texts, and before she had everything put back, the bell rang for third hour. Tossing in the rest of the mess, she grabbed her English books, slammed the locker door, and hurried down the hallway, anxious for the morning to be over.

Mrs. Vetter's car was not in the driveway when Tim dropped Annette home at twelve-thirty. Terry had ridden home with them and was sitting in the back seat.

"Looks like Mom went to work," he said.

"She probably got called in," said Annette. "But at least she has tomorrow off."

"When do you leave for the lake house?" Tim kept the engine running as Annette and her brother gathered up their stuff.

"Tomorrow morning," said Annette.

"Want me to milk the cow in the morning?"

"No, just in the evening," said Annette, "and then Sunday morning, of course. Tim, I hope it's not going to be too much trouble."

"No trouble at all," he assured her with a warm smile.

Terry waited for Annette to open the door and step out. "Yeah, Tim, thanks for doing this for us. I appreciate your dad giving me the day off as well."

"No problem," said Tim. "You coming over later?"

"I'll be there at the usual time," said Terry.

Annette got out, then let her brother out. As he headed for the Vetter farmhouse, they heard Ginger barking from inside the enclosed porch. Annette leaned her head into the car and said, "Want me to call you later?"

"The usual time …" His warm smile and twinkling green eyes made her heart spin.

"Later then." She smiled as she stepped back and closed the car door.

"Later," he said, then waited till she'd started for the house before backing down the driveway.

Ginger charged out the screen door of the porch after Terry went in, and ran over to greet his favorite human. Annette crouched and gave her collie a hug as his tail swished back and forth and he licked her face.

"I love you too, Ginger," said Annette, then glancing at Tim's Chevelle as it left, she murmured, "Life is wonderful. I don't want things to change."

3

An Unexpected Visitor

That night Annette and Ruby packed their suitcases with the clothes they were taking to Minocqua. Ginger lay beside the bed on his rug, his white collie paws cradling his head as his big brown eyes watched their every move. Ruby's kitten, Clyde, was prowling around inside their room, poking her whiskers into drawers and the closet.

"It's going to be so fun staying in a lake house," Ruby said as she pulled on her nightgown while Annette sat in front of her vanity, brushing her auburn hair. "It's just too bad we can't take Ginger and Clyde with us on our spring vacation."

One of Ginger's ears twitched at the mention of his name.

Annette lurched sideways to catch Clyde, who had lost her balance while trying to climb to the top of the mirror. Ruby laughed at the cat's antics. "I really wish Mom had the week off as well," she commented. Then she sighed as she sat down on the bed. "I hope the Parkers will like me," said Ruby.

"Ruby, you have nothing to worry about," said Annette. "They'll love you as much as we do."

Ruby kicked off her slippers. "You know what's interesting?" she asked.

"What?" asked Annette.

"Have you noticed I haven't had those bad dreams anymore?"

Annette glanced at the girl on the bed. "Well, that's a good thing, Ruby. Maybe seeing Doctor Randall has made a difference."

Ruby had experienced disturbing nightmares during her first couple of months living in the Vetter household. Most of the dreams had involved the traumatic experience she'd had while living at the foster home in Colorado Springs after her mother died. She and some of the other girls the family had taken in had been molested by the retired Air Force colonel at the home. Because Terry had shown up at a critical moment, unannounced, Ruby had escaped getting hurt, but the incident had led to the two kids running away together.

"Yes, Doctor Randall is really nice," admitted Ruby, "but she doesn't believe me when I tell her that my father is alive."

Annette glanced at Ruby, who lay down and pulled the covers over herself. She put her brush on the dresser top, then went to close the bedroom door so that the hall light wouldn't disturb them. She knew Mrs. Vetter would be home from work within the hour. Annette then walked over to her side of the bed and pulled the covers back. "Do you really think he's still alive?" she asked.

Ruby sighed, pulling the covers up to her shoulders. "Well … my dream was so vivid. I feel really strongly that my dad's alive. But it's been almost two months and there's been no word."

"Sometimes we can wish so hard for something," said Annette, "that it makes it so much harder when the wish doesn't come true. What does Doctor Randall say?"

Ruby sighed again. After a long pause, she said, "She thinks I need to accept the fact that my dad's never coming home." Ruby sniffed. "Oh, Annette, I can't give up on him … I just can't."

Afraid that her sister would start crying, Annette reached her hand over and stroked a lock of Ruby's hair. "It's okay, Ruby. You just go on believing. Don't give up on him." Then she smiled as she thought of something. "You know, I never gave up on the idea that I wanted to be part of a family ... even though I lost my father when I was four years old ... and now I have you and Terry. You two are the best things that ever happened to me."

Ruby giggled then. "You mean, besides Tim."

Annette chuckled. "Tim too," she added. Suddenly, they heard Ginger on the floor let out a huge dog sigh and both of them laughed. "And Ginger, of course!" said Annette.

Clyde jumped up on the bed at that moment and started pouncing on the lumps where their feet were under the covers. Ruby squealed in delight. "Clyde! Come here!"

The kitten wasn't quite ready to settle down for the night and continued to play with both their feet as they giggled and slowly grew tired, then finally slipped off to sleep. Clyde finally relaxed and curled up on Ruby's thighs, purring softly.

The next morning, Annette was up just after the sun rose. She quietly got dressed, then went downstairs with Ginger, grabbed her jacket, and went to the barn to milk her cow, Alice. The cow had given birth to a calf in December. The sister cow, Elizabeth, had dried up and was due to have her calf in less than a month. The pregnant Holstein stood and munched hay while Annette pulled the milking stool over to do her work.

Her mind went over all the events in her recent life. A lot had happened since last summer, after she and Penny had returned from their week's vacation in Colorado. It had been Annette's first experience helping to solve a mystery while they stayed with Mandy Mitchell and her parents on their ranch outside Gunnison, in the Cochetopa Hills.

An old mountain man by the name of Jebb Hickory had been at the center of that mystery, and the Mitchells' ranch hand, Britches, had also been involved. She recalled the dangerous rockslide they'd been caught in while on horseback during a thunderstorm in the hills, and how Penny had brought home The Cheeze, the young Bratislavian sheep dog that she claimed had saved her life. Cheeze and Ginger had quickly become best dog friends.

Then the school year had started. That's when Annette had met Pete Randt, whose family had just moved onto the farm on Gaston Road. She had also met a new girl named Chris Hilgert, who had sat next to her in Art class and was a year older. Chris had brought a mystery to Ravensville involving her family, and with Annette's involvement there was more danger uncovering the cause of one murder and preventing another.

In October, Homecoming was on the girls' minds. Annette desperately wanted Pete to ask her to the dance, but then Pete's older cousin Luke showed up for an extended visit, and things didn't go in the direction Annette had hoped. Another mystery had cropped up with a drug ring threatening the local high school kids. Again, Annette was central in solving the mystery which focused on the pouting pumpkin Penny had carved for Halloween.

A freak snowstorm hit western Wisconsin on Thanksgiving. Annette and Penny had volunteered to baby-sit Pete Randt's younger brothers and sisters while his mother went to the hospital to have another baby. By then, Annette and Pete were growing closer, and due to Mrs. Randt's difficult birth, the girls volunteered to stay and baby-sit the entire weekend. In that time they solved another mystery having to do with the legend of the Man with the Lantern, and poachers in the area.

Mrs. Vetter had been dating a man named Earl Warner,

but when Annette discovered Earl had ulterior motives, she had to tell her mom. The mystery was solved, but Annette was not happy that her mother's heart was broken. By the time Christmas season arrived, Annette noticed her mother's mood worsening. They had talked about going to Minocqua to see the relatives over Christmas, but Mrs. Vetter decided she wanted to work instead.

"Last Christmas was my best one ever," Annette said out loud as she continued to milk the cow. She smiled, remembering how Terry and Ruby had come into their lives because of yet another mystery—this one involving the old abandoned ranger tower. It had also been memorable because Annette realized she was attracted to Penny's brother Tim, yet she didn't want to hurt Pete's feelings because she could see how much he liked her.

Ground Hog's Day came in early February, around the time that Ruby was having her nightmares. The Valentines Dance was coming up, where the girls asked the boys, and Annette knew Pete was expecting her to invite him. Yet she really wanted to ask Tim, but was afraid to. Tim being a senior and two years older, Annette felt she didn't stand a chance and would be turned down. And then there were Pete's feelings to consider ... until it was quite obvious that Pete was showing signs of now liking her best friend.

Annette sighed as she thought about the mystery that had taken place around Ground Hog's Day and Valentines Day. It had been that mystery involving livestock rustlers in the area that had brought to light the realization that Tim was as attracted to her as she was to him.

"Everyone's happy," murmured Annette as she finished up the milking. "I've got Tim ... and Penny's got Pete ... Ruby's dreams have stopped ... and Mom seems ..."

Annette sighed, grabbing her cloth on the bench beside her, and then the iodine. She wanted to believe that her mother was happy. After all, Mrs. Vetter had embraced the idea of having three children instead of one. She was in the process of legally adopting both Terry and Ruby. Terry, it turned out, was Annette's half brother. Ruby, for all intents and purposes, was also an orphan.

Annette had seen an improvement in her mother's life over the last three months. Still … she wasn't sure if her mother was truly happy. She didn't know if Mrs. Vetter had completely gotten over Earl Warner. At least she hadn't shown interest in any other men.

Ruby came bursting into the barn just then, dressed in a red sweatshirt and blue jeans. "Penny called," she reported. "She'll be over in an hour."

"Is Mom up yet?" asked Annette.

"Yes." Ruby grinned. "Terry too. We're going to leave as soon as we have breakfast."

Ginger stood up and shook himself, then went over to greet the younger girl.

"I'll be right in. Do you wanna feed Ginger for me?"

"Sure! Come on, Ginger," called Ruby.

Annette cleaned up and put the milk in the cooler, made sure the cows had feed and fresh water, then opened the back door for them to go out into their small pasture.

"Mooooo…"

Annette went over and rubbed Elizabeth between her black ears. She ran her hand along the cow's bulging flank. "It's gonna be all right, girl," she crooned. "Tim'll be over this evening to make sure you're taken care of."

She finished her chores, then paused at the barn door before going to the house. "My life is so good right now," she said. "I just hope nothing happens to change things." Then she went outside into the cool sunshine and headed for the house.

It was mid-morning when Will Knutson's breakfast of Pop Tarts and instant coffee was interrupted by a rapping on his front door. He was seated in his blanket-covered lawn chair in the modest, cluttered small living room of his trailer. The *Wisconsin State Journal* was spread out on his TV tray, and he had to move it aside to get out of the chair.

"Good grief, who can that be?" he muttered as he stood up and headed for the door. At least he had gotten dressed on this Saturday morning of Easter weekend.

The knocking banged louder on his door.

"*Hang on,* I'm coming!" Will shouted, annoyed at the disturbance. He figured it was probably a solicitor, or possibly that nosy elderly neighbor of his, Shirley, who loved nothing better than to collect all the court gossip and spread it around.

With a sigh he opened the door, but was surprised to find standing there a tall man in his forties, with thinning brown hair and a mustache. A scar on his right temple made his eyebrow look as if it were extended into a frown. His hands were in his pockets and he wore a thin blue jean jacket and loose beige trousers. The blue eyes pierced Will's and a crooked smile trembled across the man's face.

Speechless, Will could only stare.

"Hello, Will," the man finally said. He blinked, then the smile faded. "Can I come in?"

Stepping back, Will made room for the man to enter. He couldn't believe his eyes. As the man stepped inside the trailer, Will struggled for words. "What … you … where …" Then he shouted, "Bob! You're … Bob!"

"I would have called you, Will, but I only had an address," the man explained. Then he sighed. "I've been driving for two days … do you mind if I sit down?"

Will backed up, then looked around at his messy living room. Then he ushered Bob Foley inside and offered him another lawn chair that he had to clear off first. He scooped up the pile of newly laundered clothes he hadn't bothered to put away yet. "Please … sit down. Bob! I can't believe it's you."

Bob sank into the lawn chair and then looked around at the small accommodations.

"When did you get home?" asked Will, piling the clothes onto another TV tray in the corner. "What happened to you?" Then Will remembered his manners. "Here, let me fix you a cup of coffee. It's instant. Is that all right?"

"Instant's fine," said Bob.

Will moved over into his kitchenette area, opened a cupboard and took out the jar of Folger's and a cracked but clean mug. "I can't believe you're here. I'm sorry … I'm rather shaken at the sight of you. We all thought … I mean, we were sure you were …"

Bob said the word, "Dead?"

Will put fresh tap water into his tea kettle and set it on the stove. "You're alive!" He turned and grinned at his brother-in-law. "Bob Foley's alive! Please, tell me what happened."

"I'll be glad to. But do you mind if I wash up first?" Bob rubbed his eyes.

Will nodded toward the bathroom door. "Coffee'll be ready in a few minutes."

Bob stood up, then again looked around. "The kids aren't here?" he asked.

Startled, Will turned on the burner, then stepped toward the man. "No. They *were*. Well, I'll explain …"

Bob quickly disappeared into the bathroom, and when he emerged several minutes later, Will had set up another TV tray for the coffee and was toasting another Pop Tart.

Twenty minutes later, Bob Foley had related his story to Will Knutson, his wife's brother, and it was obvious that Bob was still in shock after learning about his wife's suicide.

"Ruth wasn't right," Will said sadly, sipping his coffee.

"I know." Bob sighed. "She had her problems."

"And, of course you had no way of knowing," Will continued. "Terry and Ruby got put into foster homes after it happened. They were in separate houses. Terry was the lucky one."

"What do you mean?" Bob asked. He hadn't touched his Pop Tart.

"Terry was living with one of his friend's parents. Ruby was put in with a retired Air Force colonel and his wife, who turned out to be … well, kind of abusive …"

"What?" Bob looked alarmed. "Will, what are you saying?"

Will quickly related the incident that had led to Terry rescuing his sister from the clutches of Colonel Yates, and how the two kids had managed to take a bus all the way from Denver to Madison and found their way to their uncle's trailer.

"Where are they now?" asked Bob.

"They're up in Ravensville," said Will. "Terry found out about his natural father."

"Oh." Bob took a sip from the cracked mug.

"Terry and Ruby are living with Helen Vetter and her daughter Annette. Tom died eleven years ago."

Bob merely nodded. "I want to see them."

"I already know that." Will cracked a smile, then said, "Your Pop Tart's getting cold."

4

The Lake House

"Are we there yet?" cried Ruby from the back seat of the Vetter car.

Terry, who was seated in the front passenger seat as Mrs. Vetter drove, swung around and grinned at his little sister, who was smirking. Annette laughed and said, "She's just kidding."

"No, I'm not," said Ruby. "I really want to know how far it is."

"Ruby, we've only come fifty miles from Ravensville," Mrs. Vetter told her, keeping her eyes on the highway ahead. "We've got another hundred to go."

"Soon we'll get to see some national forest," Annette promised. "It's beautiful driving through the Chequamegon."

Penny, who was seated in the back seat between Annette and Ruby, reached into her purse and pulled out a packet of M&M's. Ruby's blue eyes widened when she saw it. Penny tore a corner off the candy wrapper and let Ruby take some of the chocolates.

"You always come prepared," said Annette.

"Turn the radio on," Ruby called out.

"May I?" Terry asked Mrs. Vetter.

She nodded, then said, "Just keep it down. I don't care what you listen to, but I don't want to be distracted."

Terry fiddled with the dials on the dash, and soon he had tuned into a rock 'n roll station on AM, which was the only band the Vetter car had anyway. They listened to some Tommy James and the Shondelles, and then The Fifth Dimension played "Aquarius."

"Oh, I love that one," said Annette, leaning forward.

"Me too," said Penny, her green eyes dreamy as she popped a yellow M&M into her mouth.

"That *is* kind of nice," commented Mrs. Vetter and glanced at them with a smile.

"Hey, I'll take a couple of those." Terry stuck his left hand over the back seat and Penny shook some candies out for him.

"We're gonna have so much fun at the lake house," said Ruby.

Penny was singing along with the tune. *"Harmony and understanding ... sympathy and trust abounding ..."*

Annette leaned back and closed her eyes, the hum of the car's motion lulling her into a relaxed mood. She hoped she hadn't forgotten to pack anything important. Penny had remembered to bring her little Instamatic camera. Not knowing what kind of weather to expect in Minocqua this time of year, they had all brought long pants and warm jackets, but Annette had slipped in her bathing suit, just in case the water was warm enough to go swimming. Mrs. Vetter had said it was the wrong time of the year for swimming, but the fishing and boating would be fun.

It was just after 2 o'clock when they arrived at the lodge on Lake Minocqua. Annette watched as the car drew up alongside a blue station wagon and a white pick-up. The large building that met their eyes was made of logs with a long covered deck that extended across the front. There were two stories, with many windows and little log balconies scattered in four places. Large pines stood guard in the front yard, casting shadows on the green lawn that was populated with different kinds of shrubs and flower beds.

"Wow … there's the lake," said Ruby, pointing behind the lodge. They could see the water, bordered in back by groves of trees on the far side. The building shielded most of their view, but it was enough to cause excitement as Mrs. Vetter turned off the engine and they removed their seatbelts.

"Oh, I love it," cried Penny. She climbed out after Annette. Ruby had already jumped out on the other side of the car and was gazing around, her eyes and her mouth wide open.

Terry was opening the trunk to get out their suitcases when a woman approached from the entrance to the lodge. Annette immediately recognized her Aunt Marie, a small woman like her mother, with short brown hair and glasses. She had on light blue stretch pants and was wearing a mint green windbreaker. "Helen!" she called out with a big grin.

Mrs. Vetter smiled and walked over to embrace her sister. "Oh, Marie, look at you … I believe you've lost weight."

Aunt Marie laughed, then put her hands on her hips and gave Annette's mother a more careful look. "I may have dropped a couple of pounds. But look at you! Why, Helen, you're absolutely *glowing*." Then her attention was diverted to the four young people who gathered before her. "Annette darling, how are you?"

Annette gave her aunt a hug and said, "I'm super."

Mrs. Vetter reached out her arm and drew both Terry and Ruby closer. "Marie, these are my new kiddos … Terry … and Ruby."

"Ruby … what a lovely name." Aunt Marie gently embraced the girl. "I'm so happy to meet you."

"Me too," said Ruby.

"And you're a tall one," said Aunt Marie as she gave Terry a quick hug. "Welcome to the lake house … all of you."

Annette turned to Penny and drew her friend toward her aunt. "Aunt Marie, I want you to meet Penny Duncan," she said.

"Oh, *Penny* … of course! I've heard a lot about you." Aunt Marie laughed, then gave the dark-haired girl a hug as well. "I'm so happy you all could come."

A tall man had stepped out of the lodge entrance and was now approaching them. Annette waved at Uncle Joe, who was solidly built with a large nose, dark complexion and coarse black hair combed back over his forehead. His brown eyes widened as he approached the crowd. He wore a pair of large baggy blue jeans and a brown sweatshirt that was smudged with dirt and had a hole in it.

"Hello, Joe," Mrs. Vetter said warmly as he took her hand.

"Helen … glad you could make it," he said in a deep voice. He turned to Annette and smiled, then welcomed the other three.

"Well, come on in, it's kind of cool out here." Aunt Marie hugged herself, then led them all into the lodge. Annette, Penny and Ruby grabbed their luggage while Terry picked up his and Mrs. Vetter's bags, and followed everyone inside.

The lobby was expansive and woodsy in its decor, carpeted in green shag, with dark walls, lots of potted trees, and a large stone fireplace in the corner. Annette noticed lots of trophy heads from deer hanging above the sofas and comfy chairs that were scattered throughout the room, with wooden end tables and a bookcase along one wall. An antelope head and a mountain lion were mounted over the reception counter in the hallway.

"Where is Fern?" asked Mrs. Vetter.

"She drove to town to pick up some groceries," Aunt Marie said casually. "She should be getting back here soon.

Come on … I'll show you your rooms upstairs."

Ruby squeezed Annette's hand and whispered, "This is so groovy."

Penny giggled and followed the others as Aunt Marie and Uncle Joe led them up a wide, rustic staircase that led to a balcony overlooking the lobby.

"How many bedrooms are in the lake house?" asked Terry.

Uncle Joe responded. "Ten. We have eight rooms that we rent out, and then Marie, Fern and I stay on the residential wing, which is near the rooms we reserved for you." He led them down the hallway.

"Are there other people staying here?" asked Ruby.

"Actually, it's still considered off season," explained Aunt Marie. "In another month, we should be booking again."

"We do have a guest staying downstairs … a fisherman," added Uncle Joe, "but I think he's leaving tomorrow."

"Looks like we'll have the lake house pretty much to ourselves," chuckled Aunt Marie. She stopped and put her key in the door to a room.

"If you'll excuse me, I've got to finish a project I started," said Uncle Joe.

"Go ahead," Aunt Marie replied. Mrs. Vetter smiled at him, and he turned and headed back downstairs.

Aunt Marie opened the door, and the room they found themselves in was large with a window that looked out over the lake. There was a balcony from an outer door that opened on that side. The room had log walls and maroon-colored drapes. Two double beds with maroon spreads and lacey white pillowcases were against the wall on the right, and two rustic pine dressers took up another side of the room. A closet and shelves were in one corner.

Ruby gasped. "I love it!"

"Wow, this is where we're gonna stay?" cried Penny.

"You three girls will have this room," explained Aunt Marie. "Terry will be next door. And Helen, I know you and Terry are staying only tonight, but if you'd like your own room, I'll give you the suite downstairs. It has its own bathroom."

Mrs. Vetter shook her head. "Nonsense. I'll stay in this room with the girls. There's plenty of room here ... two double beds. I don't want you to have to make up another room just for me staying one night."

"It's certainly no problem," insisted Aunt Marie.

"We want Mom to stay with us," said Ruby. "Mom, you can sleep on my bed."

Penny set her luggage down and walked over to the window to look out, fascinated by the view.

"Well, okay ... but there's plenty of room."

"Thanks, Marie, but this will be fine," said Mrs. Vetter.

"Terry, come on. I'll show you your room." Marie led the tall blond boy halfway out, then turned to the rest of them and said, "The girls' bathroom is just down the hall."

Annette followed Penny and Ruby out onto the balcony and they marveled at the sparkly ripples on the lake with a crisp blue sky and fluffy white clouds. A cardinal sang from a nearby tree and a breeze swept over them.

"It's going to be too cold to swim, I'm afraid," said Penny, hugging herself. "After we unpack, I'm going to grab my jacket and let's take a walk down to the water."

"Is anybody hungry?" asked Mrs. Vetter after they had settled in a bit.

"I am," admitted Ruby.

"You mean, you're not full of M&Ms?" teased Annette.

As if in answer to the question, Terry knocked on the half opened door and stuck his head in. "Aunt Marie said there are sandwiches down in the kitchen. She's fixing some lemonade."

"Let's go," said Ruby and pulled Mrs. Vetter into the hall.

"We'll be right down," Penny told him. She turned to Annette, who was putting the last of her clothes into a drawer. "I feel so guilty, Annette."

"Why?" Annette stared at her dark-haired friend.

Penny sighed. "We're at the lake house, having fun over spring break, and poor Pete and Tim have to stay in Ravensville and work."

"Yeah, Terry and Mom, too," she added. "But you know what they say ... absence makes the heart grow fonder."

Penny giggled. "I guess we'll find out if that's true." Then she sat on the end of the bed and stared up at Annette. "I just have to know ... Annette, are you sure it doesn't upset you that Pete and I ..."

"*Pen!*" Annette frowned at her friend and crossed her arms. "Why would you ask that? You know how fond I am of Tim. Of course I'm not upset. I'm really happy for the way things turned out with us. You have Pete ... and I have Tim ... at least for now." She sighed and straightened up her bangs in the mirror.

"What do you mean, at least for *now?*" asked Penny.

Annette scowled. "It's just that ... oh, Pen, I'm having such a happy life right now. I couldn't have asked for anything better."

"Then why are you worried?"

"Well, because ... it's because ..."

Ruby barged in just then. "Come on, you two! Cousin Fern just got home. Come on downstairs. She wants to see you."

5

A Disturbing Phone Call

Ruby led the older girls downstairs and down a hallway that led to the large kitchen. They passed through a dining room that was set up with four long tables made out of pine logs, to accommodate the guests who stayed at the lodge.

The family was in the kitchen, standing around a long counter, where Aunt Marie and Annette's mother were busy putting sandwiches together. They were chatting freely while Uncle Joe washed up at the sink, and Terry took glasses down from the cupboard for the lemonade.

A tall girl with short black hair was putting food away in the oversized refrigerator. She turned around and saw Annette, and grinned. "Hi, Nettie!"

"Fern!" called out Annette. She blushed because she hadn't wanted the others to find out that ridiculous nickname Fern had pinned on her many years ago, when they were just tots.

"Fern, get some ice cubes out for Terry," Aunt Marie instructed.

"So glad you guys could come for spring break," Fern said, momentarily ignoring her mother. She was dark-complected like her dad and slender with a long neck, high cheek bones and heavy eye makeup. She swept a hand over her bangs, then reached into the freezer side to pull out a tray of ice cubes.

Terry walked over and took them from her. Then Fern closed the refrigerator door and joined the three girls at the family's kitchen table.

"This is Penny, my best friend," Annette introduced, "and you've already met my new sister Ruby."

"Yes!" Fern smiled at Penny. "You two go back a long way. I know, because whenever Nettie would come here to visit us, she'd always be talking about you."

"You have a really big kitchen," said Ruby, looking around.

Fern laughed. "That's because we have lots of guests to feed," she said. "They get their meals out in the dining room, but in here is where *we* eat."

"This is really quite a place," said Penny. "You're so lucky to live in this beautiful area."

"Yes, I like Minocqua a lot," she said. Then she asked, "Have you been down to the lake yet?"

"No, we just got here," explained Annette.

"Well, after we eat, let's go down and take a walk on the lakeshore," said Fern.

"That sounds like fun," said Ruby.

Terry brought a tray over with five lemonade tumblers. He set it down on their table, then took the empty seat between Annette and Fern. Aunt Marie brought them a plate heaped with chicken sandwiches and a bowl of green grapes. Then she joined Mrs. Vetter and Uncle Joe, who had seats at the counter.

"Oh, these look yummy." Ruby reached for a sandwich. Annette picked up her glass of lemonade and sipped it. It had just the right amount of tartness.

Penny spread a paper napkin over her lap and asked, "Do you live here year round?"

Fern nodded as she bit into a sandwich.

Annette caught bits of the adults' conversation and knew that her aunt and uncle were getting the full scoop on how Terry and Ruby had come into their lives.

"It's so cool that Annette now has a brother and a sister," said Fern. "What about you, Penny?"

"Yup ... I have a brother and a sister too." She glanced at Annette. "In fact, Annette's dating my brother."

Fern blinked at Annette. "I thought you were going with that Peter somebody ... and didn't you go to your Homecoming with his cousin?"

"She went with both of them," explained Penny.

Annette ended up having to explain to Fern how Pete's cousin Luke had invited her to Homecoming before Pete had a chance, so she ended up going with both of them.

"And now you're going with Penny's brother?" Fern's brown eyes danced with excitement.

"She's known Tim all her life," said Penny, "and she still likes him. Go figure ..."

"Well, I think that's so cool," said Fern, studying Annette.

"What about you? Do *you* have a boyfriend?" Ruby asked boldly.

Fern's eyes shifted toward her parents and then she stared at her plate after taking a bite out of her sandwich. She shook her head and mumbled, "Not really."

They ate in silence for the next few minutes. Then they heard the clatter of claws against the kitchen floor and turned to watch as an older Golden Lab dog made his way toward them, his long golden tail swaying slowly back and forth.

"You have a dog?" Ruby's face lit up as the dog approached.

Annette noticed the animal's muzzle was gray and his lanky sides showed that he was in his later years. The animal came over and sat down beside Fern's seat, and she reached down and patted the dog's head.

"Good boy, Jabbo," said Fern. "He must have been napping upstairs when you arrived."

"Jabbo's still with us," commented Annette. "I remember when he was just a puppy."

Fern laughed. "That was twelve years ago. I was just five years old when Dad brought him home."

"Oh, look, it's Jabbo," said Mrs. Vetter. At the mention of his name, the old Lab got up and slowly made his way over to receive some more petting.

"I was eight when we got Ginger," said Annette.

"Has it been that long?" asked Penny.

Annette nodded, then told Fern, "And Penny got her first dog last summer."

"Oh yes, you wrote in one of your letters that you guys brought home a sheep dog from Colorado."

"His name is The Cheeze," said Penny.

Fern chuckled. "You wanna explain to me how you came up with that name?"

They were finished eating their lunch by the time Penny told the story, in great detail, of how she had been rescued by her dog, and the miracle that had allowed her to bring him home with her to Wisconsin last August.

"Now, that's quite a story." Fern laughed.

"And I have a kitten," Ruby said. "Her name's Clyde."

"Oh, really!" Fern's eyes expanded. "And tell me, why does your girl cat have a boy's name?"

But before Ruby could tell her story, the telephone rang. Aunt Marie stood up and went over to the wall phone near the doorway to answer the call. "Parker Lake House," she said into the receiver. Everyone else continued eating their lunch. A few moments later, Aunt Marie called out in an urgent voice, "Joe!" She cupped her hand over the mouthpiece and stared at her husband.

Uncle Joe asked, "What's wrong?"

Aunt Marie took a deep breath, then held the receiver to her ear and said, "Okay, officer. We'll be here the rest of the afternoon. Yes … yes, I understand. Would you like to speak to him?" There was a suspenseful pause as Aunt Marie's eyes locked on her husband's. Then she said, "All right then. We'll be expecting you soon. Goodbye." She hung up the phone.

The kitchen had grown completely silent as everyone's attention was on Aunt Marie, who had turned rather pale. Uncle Joe stood up and made his way over to her. "What is it, Marie?"

Annette and Penny exchanged glances and Mrs. Vetter set her glass of lemonade down on the counter, waiting for Aunt Marie to say something.

"Mom … what happened?" Fern looked concerned for her mother.

Finally, Aunt Marie held her head and her lip trembled. "That was the deputy county sheriff," she said softly. "There's been an accident … a terrible tragedy …"

Fern grew alarmed. "Oh, no! It's not David, is it?"

"No, Fern," mumbled Aunt Marie. "Not David."

Uncle Joe helped his wife to her chair, where she sat down. Everyone waited to hear what else she had to say.

"Is the deputy coming here?" asked Uncle Joe. "You said …"

"There's been a drowning," Aunt Marie blurted out. "It was Leroy."

"Oh, no," cried Fern.

"When?" demanded Uncle Joe.

"Just now."

"Where?" asked Fern, coming over to her mother.

"He'd been out in the rowboat fishing … and they don't know what happened … but his body was discovered over by the swamp about half an hour ago. They don't think it was foul play, but there's going to be an investigation. Oh, Joe …" She burst into tears at that point.

Mrs. Vetter stood up and said something to her sister and brother-in-law, then came over to the table where the kids were and said, "Fern, why don't you take everyone outside for a while?"

Fern wiped her mouth, then said, "Come on."

Without questioning any further, Annette followed her cousin, Penny, Terry and Ruby out of the kitchen, then down the back hallway that led them to the rear entrance of the lake house. The news had rattled all of them from the relaxed mood they'd all just been in. Once they were out in the fresh air, they stopped a moment to breathe, and Annette asked, "Fern, who was it that drowned? Someone you know?"

"Leroy was our guest this weekend," said Fern. "He likes to go out in the boat and fish. I can't believe it … he was one of our regulars … kind of like a friend of the family. This is a terrible thing … and really bad timing." She attempted an apologetic smile, but it wasn't working.

Terry reached out and gave Fern a hug, then looked around and said, "Bummer."

"Fern, we're so sorry," said Penny.

"Yeah," added Ruby. "I know how it feels when someone dies."

Fern let out a sob and bent down to give Ruby a tight hug. "Oh, little darlin' … you are so brave. Thank you." She stood up and sniffed, then wiped her cheek. "Well, come on, let's go have a look at the shore."

Annette and Penny glanced at each other, then followed Fern as she led Terry and Ruby toward the pier in the back yard of the lake house. All of a sudden, the beautiful lake and sparkly water with the boats tied to the dock sent shivers down their spines.

A couple of motorboats and other small craft were moored at the pier. They walked to the end and stood, looking out at the water. Annette had always loved coming here. The pines that lined the opposite shore always thrilled her, and often there were ducks, coots and Canadian geese around. The breeze felt cool on her exposed skin, but there hadn't been time to go back to their room for jackets.

"Maybe we can go out in the canoe tomorrow," Fern suggested. "Terry, how long are you and Aunt Helen staying? Mom said you both have to get back home to work."

Terry explained about his two farm jobs. "We probably will leave early tomorrow afternoon," he said. "I wouldn't mind staying the week, though. I like it here."

Penny pointed to a boat out in the middle of the lake, where two people could be seen with fishing rods. "I'll bet the fish are biting," she commented.

"We have the best fishing here in Minocqua," said Fern, "and also great hunting in the fall. It's a sportsman's paradise."

"And there's skiing in the winter," added Annette.

"Yeah, Mom and Dad have discussed keeping the lake house open during Christmas and New Year's for the skiing tourists. But we kind of like to not have to deal with guests that time of year."

"I'll bet you get a lot of tourists in the summer, though," said Terry.

Fern nodded, then shaded her eyes as she gazed across the lake. They lingered awhile on the pier, and then they decided to take a short walk into the woods along the shoreline. The deciduous trees were just starting to bud out, and Annette noticed migratory songbirds were already in the North woods. She saw a red-bellied woodpecker and some nuthatches.

By the time they returned to the lake house, it was almost five o'clock. The deputy's car was just leaving the long circular driveway as they went inside. Uncle Joe was standing by himself in the great room, watching out the large picture window.

"Dad, is Mom okay?" Fern asked.

"She'll be fine," he replied. "Say, how about a campfire tonight? I was just about to go outside and get a fire started so we'll have coals." His brown eyes twinkled as he smiled at the others. "Hope you kids like roasted weenies. And I think Marie baked a cherry cobbler this morning."

"Mmmm, I can't wait," said Ruby. "Where's Mom?"

"She went up to your room. Fern, give your mother a hand in the kitchen, would you please?"

"Dad, what did the deputy say?" Fern asked.

Uncle Joe obviously did not want to discuss anything about the drowning. He cleared his throat and in a stern voice told her, "This is not the time to talk about it. Understood?"

Fern shrugged, then marched off to the kitchen. Terry left to go to his room on the first floor while the three girls trudged up the stairs toward their room with the balcony. The fresh air and walk along the lakeshore had tired them out. Annette wondered if she'd have time to catch a quick nap before supper.

How unfortunate it had been that something tragic had happened to someone the family knew even before their week of vacation had started at the lake. She hoped it would not put a damper on the rest of the week. She couldn't help sensing that the Parkers were quite upset with the death of their lodge guest. She also couldn't help being curious about the cause.

6

Weenie Roast

A beautiful sunset cast an orange-pinkish glow over the lake as the family sat in lawn chairs that circled the big fire pit in the back yard of the lake house. Uncle Joe had let the flames settle down over the hot coals after they'd had their fill of hot dogs, baked beans and fruit salad that Aunt Marie had provided.

Everyone had their jackets on as the evening had cooled down quite a bit. Frog sounds in the distance sent a thrill through Annette. She'd always cherished the croaking of frogs in springtime.

Ruby had a marshmallow on the end of a long stick and was heating it close to the coals. Over cobbler, the grownups had gotten into a discussion about the olden days, when Annette's mother and Aunt Marie had been girls, growing up in Black River Falls.

Uncle Joe, who was originally from Minocqua, had married Aunt Marie after he'd returned from fighting overseas. He had stayed in the service for a number of years, during which time they'd had David, then Fern. Since he enjoyed the outdoors so much, they decided to purchase the lake house in Minocqua, which they fixed up into the present lodge.

Terry joined in the conversation with the adults and talked about how his stepdad, Bob, had made the military his career and had been deployed to Vietnam, but was now Missing in Action. Ruby pulled in her stick and nibbled at the hot marshmallow, now melted.

"Serving one's country is an honorable mission," Uncle Joe told Terry. "It was one of the greatest experiences of my life. I'm sorry to hear about your stepdad. Even though I know the Vietnam conflict is not popular with the citizens of this country, I'm afraid it was a necessary evil to try and combat." Then he asked, "Have you considered joining up?"

"Me?" Terry hesitated before answering. "Uh ... no, sir."

"Why not?" asked Uncle Joe.

"Dad!" Fern scolded her father.

"I think it would be a good thing for every boy coming of age to take his turn serving his country."

"Hmm," said Terry. Annette sensed that her brother was not going to be influenced into doing something he didn't want to do.

Ruby spoke up then. "If Terry signed up for the Air Force, or the Army ... or anything like that, he'd have to go to Vietnam, and then maybe he'd end up like my ... my dad." She hung her head. "Then not only would I not have a father ... but I might lose my brother too."

"I think we've had enough discussion on this topic." Aunt Marie stood up and collected the dirty plates.

"Yes, let's please change the subject," said Fern. She stood up too, and called to Annette and Penny, who were just eating the last of their cherry dessert, "Hey, let's go down by the pier for a while. Want to?"

"Can I come?" asked Ruby.

"Of course," said Fern.

Annette and Penny both stood up.

"Terry?" Annette turned to see if her brother was going to

accompany them.

"No, I'll stay here with Uncle Joe," he said. "I want to hear more about his life."

Mrs. Vetter helped Aunt Marie gather up the food and things. "I'll help you clean up," she told her sister.

Annette followed the others down to the lakeshore. Darkness had descended over the lake and the moon had not yet come out. Fern had brought a flashlight and they walked out to the end of the pier and sat down to enjoy the reflection on the waves all around them.

A long and loud, eerie call erupted from somewhere, followed by a cackle. Ruby cried, "What's that?"

Fern laughed and so did Annette, who knew the sound of the common loon. "It was a bird," she said.

"Oh." Ruby giggled.

"I love the loons," said Penny. "They're so musical."

"And kind of paranormal sounding," added Fern.

"That must be why Penny likes them," said Annette.

"What kind of a bird are they?" asked Ruby.

Fern explained how the loons swam in the lake and were not ducks, but diving birds that mostly lived in the northern parts of the country.

Darkness had overtaken the orange glow of sunset. They talked about night sounds and strange birds for a while, and then Ruby said, "I see a campfire across the lake. Look," and she pointed to a tiny orange flickering light on the far shore.

"Somebody must be camping over there," said Penny.

"Yeah." Fern stared at the light and was silent as the other girls continued to discuss loons and other anomalies of the North.

"I'll bet there are Bigfoots that live up in these forests," said Penny.

"Don't scare me," warned Ruby. "I don't want to see a Bigfoot."

"Nor the Man with the Lantern." Annette chuckled, remembering how they had learned about the legend at the Randts' farmhouse when Reid Anderson, the Randts' hired hand, had told them about it.

"Oh, don't be silly," said Penny. "That legend wasn't real."

"How do you know?" teased Annette. "Maybe he roams these woods ..."

The discussion led into ghosts and then unexplained phenomena, a subject that Penny was particularly fond of. Fern was unusually quiet and just stared out at the lake.

"Hey, I just saw a shooting star," Ruby cried out, pointing into the sky, which was full of stars over the lake.

"Maybe we'll see more," said Penny.

Annette moved closer to her cousin. "Fern?"

The older girl seemed to snap out of whatever thoughts had consumed her. "Oh ... yeah, Nettie? You wanna go in?"

"Not yet," said Annette. Penny and Ruby had stood up and were walking off the pier. "Is everything all right?"

Fern hesitated, then sighed, still staring out across the lake. Her gaze seemed to be focused on that campfire that was still there, every so often wobbling a bit due to the wind. Then her cousin said, "Maybe we can go out in the canoe tomorrow. I need to check something out."

"What?" asked Annette.

"Something." Fern tried to make light of it.

"Fern, I can tell that you're kind of upset about that man ... the one who drowned?"

"Oh, yeah, I guess I am," she admitted. "Leroy's dead. I can hardly believe it."

"Did your family know him well?"

"Yeah, kinda. As I said, he was a regular here at the lake house. He was kind of a loner ... an older man who just liked to come and fish."

"That's so sad," said Annette. "I'm really sorry."

"Yes, me too," she said. "It's just so strange …"

Annette waited for her to say more. Penny and Ruby were laughing and playing along the shoreline.

Fern continued, "I suppose he had a heart attack or something. He must have just keeled over inside the boat and fell into the water."

Annette didn't know what else to say. Fern glanced once more across the lake at the burning campfire that was starting to dim, and then she said, "Let's go back now." Annette followed her and they joined Penny and Ruby, who were feeling tired by now and ready to go inside.

Uncle Joe had set up the movie projector in the lobby, and invited everyone to watch old 8 mm movies of when Annette had been little and had been in Minocqua playing with her cousins, David and Fern. She had been ten years old, Fern twelve and David fourteen at the time. Then he showed some older movies taken of the family at an even earlier time, and Annette heard her mother gasp when she saw footage Uncle Joe had taken of the wedding reception of Mrs. Vetter and Annette's and Terry's father.

"Oh my gosh, it's Tom!" cried Mrs. Vetter.

"That's my dad?" Terry grew excited.

They saw a very young, much thinner woman with auburn hair styled on top of her head, wearing a white wedding dress and veil, dancing to polka music with a handsome man with lighter hair and a mustache. He was slender but tall, and had on a black tuxedo and bow tie. Annette's mother at her wedding reception was laughing and having the time of her life.

"Oh, Mom …" Annette crooned. "I didn't know you were ever that young."

Aunt Marie laughed out loud, and so did Uncle Joe.

There was no sound with the movies, just the rattling of the projector as it fed film through the machine, but just seeing her two parents together — on their wedding day so long ago — almost brought tears to Annette's eyes. She had seen photographs of her dad, although there weren't too many of those. But to see him lively and moving around … it was thrilling to watch.

"So that's what he looked like," said Terry, obviously as much taken in by the footage as Annette was.

Ruby giggled. "Terry, I can see you look a bit like him."

They watched movies for another half hour, and then yawns began to emerge from the younger people. Finally, Uncle Joe turned off the light to the projector but kept it running to cool down the motor before shutting it off. "Show's over for tonight," he said.

"Thank you, Joe, for sharing those," said Mrs. Vetter.

Aunt Marie turned on the light, then said, "Since it's Easter, we were planning to go to the chapel service in the morning. It's just a small gathering of people in the resort, and very informal. We'd love it if you would all like to come."

"Sure," said Mrs. Vetter. "Terry and I aren't leaving until noon anyway. We'd love to go." She turned to the young people. "Are you kids up to attending Easter service?"

Nobody objected. Everyone was tired, though, so goodnights were said and then Annette followed Penny and Ruby up to their room. Terry and Mrs. Vetter lingered a little longer. By the time her mother came up to the room, the girls were in their pajamas and ready to turn off the light.

"I wish you were staying longer, Mom," said Ruby. "Do you really have to go home and go to work?"

Mrs. Vetter smiled as she went to her suitcase to find her robe. "I think you'll have more fun without me," she said, to which all three girls objected. She sighed, then said, "You just concentrate on having a good time during your spring break.

Promise?"

"Okay, we will," said Ruby.

"Good night, girls." Mrs. Vetter reached for the lamp switch and the room went dark.

Annette yawned. She knew she'd be asleep as soon as her head hit the pillow. "See you in the morning," she said, and snuggled in beside Penny, who was already sound asleep.

7

Penny Saves Easter

Easter morning dawned with a rosy sunrise. Bob Foley had the address that Will had written down for him on the back of an envelope, which he placed on the seat beside him. He started up the engine of his old beater of a car and was glad to see he still had almost a full tank of gas. Most people were still asleep in the trailer park as he backed out of the driveway where he'd parked next to Will's yellow station wagon. He shifted into gear and headed for the main highway.

Will had also given him the Vetters' telephone number, but when they'd tried to call last evening, there had been no answer. He'd tried again before leaving Will's trailer, but again no one had answered the phone. Will had offered to keep trying throughout the day. He'd let Helen know that Ruby's father was back from Vietnam and was on his way to Ravensville.

Bob's memory was still foggy at times, but he had finally recalled that his wife, Ruth, had been married to Tom Vetter before him, and had gotten an annulment shortly after their marriage. She had given birth to Terry, Tom' son. Ruth never told Tom about the baby. Bob had loved Ruth and raised the boy as his own. Although Terry had been told—when he was a little older — that Bob was not his real father, Ruth had insisted that he not find out about Tom. Bob had never questioned why, but respected his wife's wishes.

Ruth had been a loving wife for the first years of their marriage. She had given birth to Ruby three years later. But then his wife developed a drinking problem and it began to affect the family. Being in the Air Force, Bob's job meant he had to move his family around a lot, from base to base, and sometimes he was gone for long periods of time. Ruth had felt insecure and, unfortunately, she had found comfort in substances such as alcohol that altered her moods.

The kids had suffered most because of it. Often Ruth would accuse Bob of being too strict with the kids. She didn't like how his military background influenced how he disciplined Terry and Ruby. She especially didn't like him criticizing her drinking, and whenever he brought it up, a fight would break out between them. Bob soon sought opportunities to go on missions.

He had been recruited into a few undercover operations which he was under orders not to discuss, not even with his wife or family members. He had acquired a high national security level with his job and enjoyed the challenges that came with it, and soon saw his military career overshadowing the dysfunctional family life that only seemed to worsen.

Although he was already forty when he was deployed to Vietnam, he went and was a part of Operation Ground Hog. His memory was still foggy about the details, and even though he was able to remember more of the plane crash and his capture with his pilot, Lieutenant Bill Crawford, Bob only saw bits and pieces in his mind. Some of the horrific events that involved torture and suffering while in the Viet Cong prison camp were permanently wiped from his memory. At Walter Reed Hospital they had told him not to worry about the memory loss as it was probably a blessing. Unfortunately, his injuries had left him disabled to some extent.

He got onto the highway and headed north. He'd have to make an unannounced visit to the Vetter farm just outside Ravensville. With any luck, he'd arrive by mid-morning.

"We didn't bring any dresses," said Ruby that morning after they'd gotten up. "How can I go to church without wearing a dress?"

"I don't think it matters," said Annette as she dug through her suitcase to find a decent pair of pants and her dressiest T-shirt.

Mrs. Vetter had already gone downstairs to help Aunt Marie with breakfast. Penny came through the door after returning from the bathroom down the hall. "Did you two go out on the balcony yet?"

"Pen," said Annette, "none of us brought anything decent to wear to the chapel this morning."

"I'm wearing my jeans," she announced.

"Will anyone care?"

"From what Fern said, the resort chapel is very casual. It's for campers and lodge guests like us. Nobody cares if you're not wearing a skirt." She sat on the bed and brushed her hair. "Aunt Marie said it was informal."

"Breakfast!" they heard Fern calling from the stairway.

"Okay!" Ruby called back. All three hurried into their clothes.

Aunt Marie had prepared a spread, which she served on the sideboard in the large dining room where guests usually ate. Since there were no lodge guests this weekend, everyone was going to have breakfast in the big room. They had boiled eggs, ham slices, strawberries and grapes, link sausages and gravy with biscuits.

Annette was relieved that the dark cloud of shock and grief had lifted somewhat after yesterday afternoon's tragic news about Leroy. Fern, however, seemed to be a little moody this morning and didn't say much. She yawned quite a bit and didn't add to the conversation at the table.

At ten o'clock Uncle Joe led them on foot outside and down the lane just a few hundred yards. The chapel was a small, nondescript building, and a dozen or so people had gathered. The Parker family appeared to know every one of them as they went inside and took seats on folding chairs. The preacher was an elderly man with a rough, curly white beard and spectacles. He was dressed casually in a sweatshirt and sweatpants and wore a cross around his neck.

"Pastor Lewis, we have visitors," said Uncle Joe as he approached the minister. "I'd like you to meet Helen and her kids. They're from Ravensville."

"Nice meetin' you." The pastor smiled and shook everyone's hand. "Where's Ravensville? Not sure I've heard of it."

"I'm not surprised," Mrs. Vetter chuckled. "It's in Jackson County, half an hour or so from Black River Falls."

Everyone took seats, and Annette noticed that people were looking around the big open room, as if they were waiting for something ... or someone. The minister lit the candles and kept glancing at the doorway. The congregation began chattering in low voices.

"Where is Mrs. Lourdes?" a skinny woman with light-colored hair piled up on her head like a honeycomb asked the minister.

"Well, I ..."

Just then a young woman with dark hair, carrying a baby, came through the door and immediately went up to speak to the pastor. Then he turned to the congregation as the woman and her child took seats near the front.

"I'm afraid Sara Lourdes was feeling ill this morning," he announced to the group.

Aunt Marie leaned over and said, "Sara's the musician.

She plays the piano for services."

All kinds of moans and sighs came from the people seated. "That's too bad," a man said. "She had special music prepared for the Easter service."

"There's no music," Fern whispered to Annette and Penny.

After more murmurings and people starting to talk louder, the minister raised his hands and said sadly, "Well, it's truly a shame that we can't celebrate this beautiful holiday without Sara's lovely piano ... I guess we'll have to carry on the best we can." He picked up his Bible on the lectern and started thumbing through his notes.

Unexpectedly, Penny stood up and took two steps forward. "I'll be happy to fill in," she said.

There was a murmur in the crowd and the minister stared at the dark-haired girl.

Annette grinned and called out, "Penny plays the piano. She's really good."

"Well, I can try at least," said Penny.

Suddenly, the room erupted in light applause, encouraging Penny to volunteer her talent. The minister smiled at her and motioned her toward the piano, which faced the audience off to the left of the lectern. Penny walked over and sat down, then started arranging the music sheets that had been left for the service this morning. Then, with a smile, she stared at Pastor Lewis and he turned back to his flock and said, "Let us pray ..."

Half an hour later, after the service ended, Annette followed the others out of the chapel as Penny played her favorite Beethoven piece, the Adagio from the *Sonata Pathétique*, which she had memorized for a recital not long ago. The people shuffled out of the building slowly, enchanted with the music and speaking softly as they shook hands with Pastor Lewis and greeted others that they knew.

"Penny, you saved Easter!" cried Fern with a grin when Penny came out of the chapel.

"Your playing was lovely," said Aunt Marie.

"Thank you, young lady," Pastor Lewis said. "Everyone appreciated what you did."

Penny received lots of praise from other members as they made their way out of the yard and walked down the lane back toward the lake house.

"I didn't know you played so well," Terry said.

Ruby smiled and said, "I didn't hear any mistakes."

Penny's green eyes grew wide and she said, "I made plenty of them."

"Well, nobody cared about that," added Mrs. Vetter. "You did a fine job, Penny."

"Yes, you did," agreed Annette and squeezed her friend's hand.

When they got back to the lodge, Mrs. Vetter and Terry got ready to leave for Ravensville. It was already eleven-thirty and they needed to gas up and get headed back down the highway before noon, in order for Mrs. Vetter to get to work on time.

"Dad, can I take the girls out in the canoe?" Fern asked after Terry and Mrs. Vetter went to get their luggage.

"When?"

"Can we go now?"

"What about lunch?" asked Aunt Marie.

"We had such a big breakfast," said Fern.

"How long will you be out?" asked Uncle Joe.

"I don't know. I just want to paddle around the lake. We should be back within the hour," said Fern. Annette noticed her cousin was rather apprehensive.

"Oh, let them go, Joe," said Aunt Marie. "It's all right."

"Okay then," said Fern's father. "Just wear those life jackets."

Jabbo, the Golden Lab, had come out of his sleeping area to greet them. His long hard tail waved back and forth slowly as he went first to Ruby, who squatted down to give the old dog a hug. "Maybe I'll stay here and play with Jabbo," said Ruby.

"You don't want to go for a ride in the canoe?" asked Annette.

Ruby shook her head no. "I'm kind of tired today anyway."

It had been going on nine o'clock that morning when Bob Foley arrived in Ravensville. He had become confused and taken a wrong exit, ending up in Black River Falls. But he had turned around and gotten back on the right road to the small rural town.

Ravensville was actually larger than he'd expected. The town had a main street with several stores and businesses. There was a good-sized high school with its football field, and even a hospital. He felt at ease in this friendly place, which was so different from the more municipal Colorado Springs.

He found Ogden Road, which turned off the highway on the south side of town. He passed Browns' Country Store on the corner as he drove slowly on down the paved rural road. He noted plenty of trees on the flat terrain, and there were a few farmhouses on either side. Eventually he passed a large dairy farm on the left that had a huge barn with fenced pastures, small rolling hills, and a large white farmhouse. He slowed down to read the name on the mailbox and saw that the place belonged to the Duncan family.

A young white sheep dog that had been lying on the front porch stood up, having seen the car, and started barking at him. Bob drove on. Woods surrounded him on both sides of the road now as Ogden Road curved slightly to the left, and after a quarter of a mile, he came across the house he had been looking for.

Through the trees he could see a small, two-story farm-house, pale gray in color, with a screened-in back porch near the end of the long, narrow driveway. On the north side of the house was a garden area, an A-frame chicken house, and farther back against the woods was a good-sized red barn with a small fenced pasture attached.

Bob saw the name on the mailbox at the entrance to the driveway and smiled with relief. Will's careful directions had guided him to the Vetters' house. It looked as if they were home because there was a vehicle parked in the driveway—a blue Chevelle sports car.

Bob turned into the driveway and pulled his old beater up and parked beside the Chevelle. He didn't get out right away. Anxiety had struck. Any moment now, he realized, Terry or Ruby could come outside and they'd see him. But Will had promised to keep calling the Vetters, to tell them he was coming. Would they recognize him right away? Would his sudden appearance be a shock? How was he going to handle this reunion with his children after so many months away from them?

No longer able to bear the suspense, Bob pushed the door handle down and slowly got out of the car. Immediately he was greeted with fresh, invigorating springtime air that filled his lungs. Moist woods smell greeted his nostrils with just a hint of cow smell. He noticed there were no chickens in the little poultry area and things were very quiet. Certainly the family was up by now, unless … well, it was always possible they had gone to Easter church services. He had noticed lots of cars and people in the parking lots of the small churches he had passed in town.

He started limping toward the house, wondering if he should go around to the front entrance or be bold and knock on the back door. His muscles were a little stiff from the long drive, so his limp was worse than usual. He was halfway to the porch when he heard a dog bark.

Turning to his right, he saw a red collie at the barn door. A man ... or actually, it looked like a teen-aged boy ... was coming out of the barn. He had dark wavy hair and wore coveralls. The young man had seen Bob and stopped to stare. The dog continued to bark and wag its tail.

Bob waited while the teen-ager and the collie approached him. There was a puzzled look on the boy's face as he wiped his hands on the front of his coveralls. "Hello ... what can I do for you?" the young man called out.

"Is this the Vetter place?" Bob asked.

"Yeah." The young man turned to silence the collie by putting his hand gently around its snout. "It's okay, boy. Okay ..."

Bob offered his hand. "I'm Bob Foley," he said.

"Tim Duncan." Tim shook the tall man's hand, still curious about him.

"You work here?" Bob asked.

"Nah ..." Tim smiled. "I'm just helping out for the day. "Are you a friend of Helen's?"

Bob rubbed his mouth and shook his head. "Are Terry and Ruby here?" he finally asked. There was a quiver in his voice and he glanced over at the silent house while the collie bent closer and sniffed Bob's shoe.

"Actually, no," said Tim. "They all went up north to the lake house."

"Lake house?" Bob looked puzzled.

Tim explained, "It's spring break. They drove up yesterday to visit some relatives of the Vetters."

"Oh." Bob sighed, disappointed.

"Wait ..." Tim tilted his head as he looked Bob in the eye. "What did you say your name was again?"

"Foley. I'm Bob Foley, the kids' dad."

Tim grew excited. "You're Ruby's father!"

"That's right," said Bob.

"But ... we thought ... we all thought you were ... weren't you in Vietnam?"

Bob nodded his head. "I was." Then he smiled. "But I'm back."

"Gad ..." Tim looked around the yard, pondering what to do.

"I tried calling them," said Bob. "Nobody answered." He then told Tim how he'd driven all the way from Colorado and spent last night at Will Knutson's trailer in Madison. Then he asked, "Do you have a phone number where I can reach them?"

Tim shook his head. He noticed the man's scar on the right side of his forehead and the way he held his arm. He had also noticed how he limped from his car toward the house. "I don't," he admitted. "They didn't leave a number. All I know is they went to Minocqua."

"Where's that?" asked Bob.

"Minocqua? Up north," said Tim, "about a two-hour drive ... maybe longer."

"Where are they staying?"

"I'm not sure. They said something about a lake house ... Helen's sister and her husband run a lodge. They were going to spend the week there."

"How do I get to Minocqua?" asked Bob.

Tim told him to get on Highway 50 and keep heading north.

"I'll find it." Bob cleared his throat, patted the dog's head, then limped back toward his car.

"Well, okay," said Tim, still a bit in shock and wondering how the family was going to react when they realized Bob Foley was alive.

Bob swung into his beater, cranked up the engine, then

backed down the driveway before Tim could think clearly again. It wasn't until Bob was speeding back up Ogden Road toward the highway that Tim remembered Terry and Mrs. Vetter were coming back that afternoon. In fact, Mrs. Vetter had to work at the hospital at three o'clock. Why hadn't he thought to tell Bob they'd be returning today?

Ginger sat down on the grass and dug at an itch on his side. Tim crouched down and ran his hand through the collie's beautiful white mane. "Well, come on, Ginger. Get in the car. Let's go home." He opened the door to the Chevelle and the collie jumped inside.

"It's going to be an interesting week for Annette," Tim chuckled as he climbed into his car. "I wish I could be there to see the look on her face."

Ginger sat in the passenger seat and stuck his pointy head out the window as Tim's car swung around and left.

8

Bad Luck

Within half an hour of getting home from the chapel, Mrs. Vetter and Terry were packed up and ready to drive back south to Ravensville. Aunt Marie insisted on sending along a container of hot cross buns she had baked for Easter. It was noon by the time Annette waved at her mother and brother and they drove away from the lake house.

"Such a beautiful day," Penny remarked as she walked with Annette and Fern to the pier. They had all changed into more suitable clothing. Although the sun was out and it was springtime, the air was still cool and required them to take their jackets or sweatshirts as Fern, carrying a knapsack, led them to the family's canoe that was tied up to the dock.

Annette had tried to talk Ruby into going for a ride in the canoe with them, but the girl had declined once again. "Maybe next time," she'd said with a smile. She had made friends with Jabbo, and Annette figured her little sister just needed some time to reflect. After all, Ruby had been through a lot in the last few months and she was just starting to emerge from that dark place following the loss of her parents and her abuse at the foster home.

"Is Ruby feeling okay?" Fern asked as they climbed into

the canoe and put on their orange life jackets.

"I think so," said Annette. "You know, she's still getting over the loss of her mother."

"And her father," added Penny, buckling her jacket.

"I can't imagine how that feels," said Fern, "having a member of your family Missing in Action." Then she asked, "Is there any possibility he could still be alive?"

Annette and Penny glanced at one another, then Annette said, "Probably not. But Ruby keeps hoping he is."

"Tell Fern about Ruby's dreams," prompted Penny, her green eyes expanding.

"Dreams? What dreams?" asked Fern.

Annette told her cousin about the nightmares Ruby had started having in January, after she had come to live in Ravensville with them. "They seem to have stopped finally," she concluded. "I think Ruby's coming along fine."

"You didn't tell her about that dream Ruby had of her father," Penny reminded Annette.

"Actually, she had a *few* dreams about her dad ... over in Vietnam," said Annette.

Fern looked interested. "Like what?"

"She kind of heard him talk to her ... in her dreams," said Penny, who loved talking about subjects that were extraordinary. "She even believes her dad is alive and is coming home to her."

Nobody said anything more. They soon were drifting out toward the middle of the lake. Fern paddled on one side while Annette paddled on the other. For a few minutes they were silent, basking in the beauty of the lake, the blue sky and white clouds, the pines lining the lakeshore on all sides, with a distant cabin roof popping into view every now and then.

"I'll be glad when David gets home from Vietnam," Fern spoke up as they were about halfway across the lake.

"Your brother?" asked Penny.

"Yes," said Fern, "he's in the Marines, like my father was."

"Did he get drafted?" asked Annette. "I can't remember."

"No, he volunteered," explained Fern, "but if he hadn't, I'm sure they would have drafted him."

"Tim just turned eighteen," said Penny. "Gosh, I hope it doesn't happen to him."

Annette shuddered, thinking of Tim. She knew that he had done his duty and signed up for Selective Service after his birthday the end of January. But now the fact that he had been accepted into college meant the chances of being drafted and sent to war were greatly reduced.

"Tim's your boyfriend?" Fern smiled at Annette with a twinkle in her brown eyes.

"Yes," Annette murmured, trying to hide her smile. Sometimes she could hardly believe it was true, yet it was. She just hoped …

"I hope you guys don't mind." Fern interrupted Annette's thoughts. "I want to paddle over to the far shore and check on someone." She began to paddle faster so that Annette had to work a little harder to keep up.

"I certainly don't mind," said Penny, who didn't have a paddle.

"Me neither," added Annette, then asked, "Who is it?"

Fern didn't look at her. She just said, "You'll see."

M rs. Vetter and Terry had driven half an hour since leaving the lake house, when Terry noticed something wasn't right. "Mom, what's that bouncing sound?" he asked.

"I don't know," she replied. "I thought it was just the pavement."

"No," he said, looking concerned. "I think there's something wrong with the car."

"Goodness," said Mrs. Vetter, glancing over her left

shoulder. "I'm going to pull over."

Terry pointed out the window. "I think I see a service station ahead on the right."

"Oh, good," said Mrs. Vetter, who had also noticed they were on the northern outskirts of Tomahawk.

"I think we might have a flat tire," said Terry.

Mrs. Vetter let out a sigh. Now that he had mentioned it, the thumping sound that she thought had been uneven road was increasing. She slowed the car down and signaled to let other drivers know she was getting over into the right shoulder of the road. They slowed even more, and the Vetter car finally rolled into the parking lot of the gas station, where a couple of cars were getting gasoline, and there were customers going into the store part of the station.

"Do you think anyone will be around to fix a flat tire on Easter?" Mrs. Vetter cried.

"I don't know," said Terry. "We'll find out."

"Oh, why did this have to happen now?" she fretted as the car rolled to a stop in front of the garage. "Let's pray there is someone here who can help us."

Almost immediately a man in navy blue coveralls and a dark blue cap stepped out from the station door and saw them. He came right over with a smile on his face. "Looks like you've got a flat," he remarked.

Terry was already out of the car. Mrs. Vetter grabbed her purse and climbed out on the driver's side. The station mechanic and Terry were examining the front right tire, which was quite flat and made that side of the car tilt a bit.

"Don't worry, ma'am," the attendant said with a smile. "We'll get your tire off and repaired, and soon you'll be on your way." He seemed cheery enough, and Terry helped him after he went to get the jack out of his shop.

Mrs. Vetter realized this unfortunate delay was going to make her late getting to the hospital for her shift. She crossed her arms and stood in front of the car, wondering what to do. Terry and the mechanic finally were able to get the tire off the wheel, and Terry said to Mrs. Vetter, "Mom, why don't you wait inside and get a cup of coffee or something?"

"How long is this going to take?" she asked.

The mechanic smiled apologetically. "Half an hour ... maybe less. Depends on what caused the flat."

"Will I have to purchase a new tire?" she asked. She hadn't brought a lot of money along on the trip.

"I'll know soon enough," said the mechanic and beckoned to Terry. "Come on, young fella. You're welcome to come in the shop and give me a hand."

"Sure," said Terry, then turned and shrugged.

"Okay," said Mrs. Vetter. "I'm getting some coffee, and then I'll need to call work." Without waiting for a reply, she walked over to the front of the station, where the gas pumps were and people were coming and going on this holiday after-noon. As she walked into the store, she noticed there was a pay phone outside near the restrooms.

Five minutes later, she came out with a Styrofoam cup of coffee, to which she'd added some creamer. She noticed there was a man in the phone booth, so she waited in front of the gas station, sipping some of the hot coffee, trying not to burn her tongue.

Another five minutes passed as she watched people and station attendants filling gas tanks, washing the windshields and checking engine oil in their customers' cars. Glancing over at the phone booth, she saw that the man was still in there. What was he doing? He didn't seem to be talking on the tele-phone.

Finally, Mrs. Vetter sighed and walked over to the phone booth. The man inside was tall with thin brown hair and a mustache. He wore a blue jean jacket and was paging through the phone book. Parked next to the booth was a rusty old Ford

Falcon that had seen better days. The paint was rusting and there were scratches, dents, and a cracked windshield. She hesitated, but then knocked on the door of the phone booth.

The man turned around and looked at her with curious blue eyes, then opened the door to talk to her. "Ma'am?"

"How long are you going to be?" asked Mrs. Vetter. "I need to make a call."

"Oh … oh, I'm terribly sorry." The man fumbled a bit with the phone book, which had also seen better days and was a bit mutilated from use. "I'm sorry," he said. He put down the phone book and stumbled as he emerged from the booth.

Mrs. Vetter immediately noticed that the man, who looked about forty, was lame. He had a scar across his right forehead and he held his arm in an unnatural position. As he fell forward, having lost his balance, she reached out and caught him. Without much effort, he straightened himself and regained his dignity with an attempt at a smile.

"Thank you," he mumbled, then moved toward the old car. He motioned for Mrs. Vetter to go ahead and use the phone while he waited.

Digging through her purse, Mrs. Vetter found some change and deposited them into the slot, then made her call to Ravensville General Hospital. "Third floor, please."

One of the nurses from the day shift answered, and she explained her dilemma. "I'm afraid I'm going to be an hour late to work. It can't be helped. I'm having some bad luck. The car got a flat tire."

"I'll tell the head nurse when she comes in. Helen, don't worry about it. Just drive home safely."

"I will. Thanks. Goodbye." Mrs. Vetter hung up, then closed up her purse and stepped out of the phone booth to find the tall, brown-haired man leaning against his car, watching her. It startled her for a moment, but then she smiled in a friendly fashion. "Thank you, sir."

He didn't answer right away, but his eyes had locked with hers. She found herself momentarily suspended, then took in a quick breath and turned to go back to the gas station store and wait for Terry and the mechanic to finish with the tire.

"I hope you have a wonderful afternoon," the stranger called after her. His voice had an unusual soothing quality.

Mrs. Vetter glanced back and felt a flush of embarrassment. "Why ... thank you." Then she added, "I hope you do too."

He smiled, then slowly limped back inside the phone booth while she hurried to get inside the station. Her heart was racing and she felt flustered for some reason. She couldn't understand what it was about the man that had rattled her. Usually she wasn't attracted to strange men. Being a nurse, she had been there to keep him from falling and hurting himself. Yet, there had been a certain look on his face ... a kindness and gentleness in those blue eyes ... and he wasn't bad looking, even with the scar.

Once she got back inside the store, she found herself peeking out the window in the direction of the phone booth, where the man appeared to be browsing again through the battered phone book.

When she finished drinking all the coffee in the Styrofoam cup, she walked over to the trash can and dropped it in, then visited the ladies' room and replenished her lipstick. By the time she came out, Terry was in the store looking around for her.

"Oh, there you are, Mom." He grinned. "All set. The tire's fixed."

"Thank goodness," said Mrs. Vetter.

Together they walked out to the car, where the mechanic was just finishing up as he tightened the lug bolts one last time. Mrs. Vetter happened to notice that the tall man in the phone booth was no longer there, and his Ford Falcon was gone as well.

"Now you can get back on the road," said the mechanic after Mrs. Vetter paid him. "Your son was a big help."

Terry smiled and got into the car. "I didn't do anything," he murmured. "Did you call the hospital?" he asked.

"Yes," said Mrs. Vetter. "Everything's good." She smiled as she started up the engine.

9

Hiding Out

Fern steered the canoe over to some tall grasses against the shore on the opposite side of the lake. With her paddle, Annette helped pull them against the bank as Fern climbed out into the shallow water, hanging onto the boat as it bobbed against the waves.

Penny looked into the woods area and said, "I guess we're getting out." Then she carefully emerged from the craft onto the bank.

Annette tucked her paddle into the bottom of the canoe, then climbed onto the weedy shore and helped her cousin pull the canoe up onto dry ground. She looked around and noticed right away a campfire pit in a small area that had been cleared of smaller pine trees and other growth.

"It's just a short walk in this direction," Fern told the other girls. She grabbed her knapsack out of the bottom of the canoe. They left the canoe and started walking into the woods.

"This is so gorgeous," remarked Penny with a big smile. "I love it here."

"It's so different from our woods back home," Annette had to admit. "You have such tall evergreens here. Our woods are mostly deciduous."

"And the smell ..." Penny drank in large gulps of air as they walked. "I love the smell of pine."

"Me too," said Fern.

"Where are you taking us?" Annette asked.

After a moment of silence, Fern said without looking at them, "I wanted to have you meet my friend."

Soon a little cottage came into sight. Annette noticed it was more of a shack than anything else. It may have once been somebody's cottage, but there were broken windows and some of the logs on the side were rotting and lacked stain.

Annette and Penny looked at one another but didn't say anything. As they grew nearer, a door on the side of the shack opened and a young man with long, scraggly dishwater blond hair stepped outside. He had on a brown hooded sweatshirt and blue jeans with patches. He was fairly tall and appeared to be trying to grow a beard and mustache. He wore glasses and grinned when he saw them coming.

"Hi, Aaron," Fern called to him. "It's all right. This is my cousin Nettie and her friend Penny."

Aaron waved at the girls, and then Fern led them right up to him. "Cool," he said with a friendly smile. He reached his hand out to Penny, who smiled and shook it. "Penny?"

"Yes," she replied.

Then he turned to Annette. "And glad to meet you, Nettie."

"Please ... call me Annette," she begged. "I've long outgrown that nickname." Then she turned to Penny with a warning look. "And don't you dare tell Tim."

Penny only giggled as she looked at her surroundings, fascinated by it all.

"I brought you something." Fern reached into her knapsack and brought out a packet wrapped in aluminum foil, and handed it to Aaron. "We had a barbecue last night."

Aaron accepted the food and unwrapped a corner of it.

"Wow … thanks, Fern." He cocked his head, then looked at the girls and asked, "Would you like to come inside?"

"We can stay out here," Fern said quickly. "Let's sit outside and enjoy the sun."

Penny looked around. "Is this your place?" she asked.

Aaron led them over to his patio area, which was just a spot on the ground next to the shack where he had placed several rocks and some old tree trunks to sit on. "I'm caretaking the place," he said, then sat on the ground and began unwrapping the hot dogs that Fern had saved for him. He wasted no time starting to eat and appeared to be hungry.

"The campfire we saw from across the lake," said Penny, indicating the pit near the lakeshore. "Was that yours?"

Aaron nodded his head, his mouth full. "I saw your campfire over at the lake house," he said. He chewed, then swallowed and added, "I was sending a greeting to Fern."

Fern looked at Annette and Penny, and then smiled apologetically. "Aaron and I met a couple of weeks ago."

Surprised, Annette managed a smile. Penny blinked, then said, "Well, that's … great."

"Her father doesn't think so," Aaron replied and wiped his chin with the back of his hand.

"He doesn't know you," Fern told him.

"Do your parents know about Aaron?" Annette asked.

"I'm not telling them," said Fern.

"Hey, the cops were over in the lagoon area yesterday," Aaron said, his gray-green eyes wide. "Do you know what that was all about?"

"As a matter of fact …" Fern sighed. "Leroy's dead."

"Leroy?" Aaron stared at her. Then he seemed to remember. "Oh … the fisherman guy you had over at the lake house."

"Yeah," said Fern. "He drowned." Her voice faltered a little.

"What happened?" asked Aaron.

Fern shrugged. "We don't know."

"Aw ... that sucks," said Aaron. "Well, I thought maybe the cops were after those dudes that reportedly broke into the Phelps cottage."

"I didn't hear about that," said Fern, growing suddenly alert.

"Yeah, some dudes have been hangin' around the lake this last week. I think it was probably them who broke in and stole some stuff. The Phelps weren't there, of course, but the neighbor saw some suspicious behavior and called the cops."

"We didn't hear about that," said Fern. "Were they caught?"

"No." Aaron pushed his glasses up a little, then started into his second hot dog.

"Who are they? Do you know? Did you see them at all?"

Aaron waited to get half his hot dog eaten, then wiped his chin again and looked her in the eye. "They came pokin' around the cabin a few days ago. There's three of 'em, I think — a girl and two guys ..."

"Hippies?" asked Penny.

Aaron shook his head. "Not really. More like agitators."

"Agitators?" Annette repeated.

"Why would you say that?" asked Fern.

"Well," said Aaron, opening the foil packet more and discovering some cherry cobbler at the bottom. "I say that because ... they asked me what I was doing here." He sniffed. "I told 'em, and they thought I should join 'em. Said they were from Chicago and had been in some of those anti-war demonstrations ... you know, Students For a Democratic Society."

"I've heard of them," said Penny. "My parents say they're trouble."

"They caused some riots in Madison, I remember," said Annette. "It was in the papers."

"They're radicals," said Aaron and started eating the cobbler. "I didn't want anything to do with them."

"Well, did they harass you?" asked Fern.

"Kinda," he admitted. "I think they're hiding from the authorities. The girl's boyfriend was arrested and was supposed to show up at a court hearing. So they split. They're drifters."

"That's awful," said Penny.

"I didn't hear anything about that," said Fern.

"Well, hopefully they've moved out of the area," said Aaron.

"We'd probably better get back to the lake house." Fern stood up and brushed off her pants.

"Thanks for the food." Aaron stood up and gave Fern a quick hug, then turned to Annette and Penny. "Nice meeting the two of you."

They left then, and when Annette glanced back at the shack, Aaron was going inside. She wondered what he was really doing there. She didn't believe he was a caretaker, and he was obviously hungry. He didn't seem that old either.

When they got back to the canoe and were heading back across the lake, Annette asked Fern about the long-haired young man. "Is he your boyfriend, Fern?"

"Yes, but please don't say anything when we get back to the lake house," she begged. "I can't tell my parents about Aaron."

"Why not?" asked Penny.

"He's a draft dodger," Fern told them.

"Oh," said Annette. Most draft dodgers she'd heard about usually headed for Canada or some other country, to avoid being drafted into the armed forces and sent to the war in Vietnam. So apparently Aaron was hiding out in the shack in the woods.

"Dad will turn him in," Fern added. "Draft dodgers

infuriate my father."

"Where is Aaron from?" asked Annette.

"Oshkosh," said Fern.

"Well, we won't say anything," said Penny.

"No, your secret's safe with us," added Annette, but she had a feeling that there was something more that Fern wasn't telling them.

It was late afternoon when Bob Foley decided to stop. He'd reached Minocqua an hour and a half earlier and had driven around town, then checked out some of the resorts. He hadn't realized there was more than one lake—there were several, in fact—and he had no idea where to find Terry and Ruby. The young man who had come out of the barn at the Vetter farm hadn't been able to give him enough information. All he had mentioned was a lake house.

"But which lake?" he wondered, pulling his car into an old motel parking lot on the edge of town. He needed to get a good night's sleep and then resume the search tomorrow. He would have slept in his car somewhere, but it was still cold out in northern Wisconsin. He needed a hot meal too, but a cup of coffee and a sandwich would have to do. He had to watch what he spent.

Mrs. Vetter and Terry found everything in order when they got back to Ravensville. Terry checked the barn and found his sister's cows contented. The one named Alice would need milking in a couple more hours, but he had to get over to the Duncan farm and help out in the milking parlor there first. Mrs. Vetter got ready and left for work at the hospital.

When Terry walked over to Duncans', he found Ginger ecstatic to see him. Tim had kept the collie at their farm so that Penny's dog, The Cheeze, could keep Annette's dog from being lonely. They had decided that since Terry would be working at both the Duncans' and for Mr. Randt on Gaston Road, Ginger could stay with Penny's family until the girls got home from their spring break.

"Hello, Terry," called Audrey Duncan from the front porch. She had a dish towel in her hand as she stood at the door. "Ray and Tim are waiting for you in the barn. The milking machine is on the fritz again. I'm sure they'll be relieved to see you."

"Thanks, Mrs. Duncan." Terry gave Ginger's red head a pat, then ran off to the barn.

10

A Close Call

R uby spent the afternoon by herself. She had taken the Parkers' Golden Lab, Jabbo, for a short walk in the woods. The old dog loved being there, smelling all the scents he found in the woods, but she noticed he grew tired quickly. She ended up taking Jabbo back to the lake house after about twenty minutes. Jabbo climbed into his dog bed with a big sigh after drinking half his bowl of water.

A sheriff's deputy had come back to the lake house to clean out the room downstairs that the Parkers' lodge guest, Leroy, had occupied. Aunt Marie had gone into the room with him, and Ruby couldn't hear the conversation, but the deputy was asking her questions. Uncle Joe appeared to be deep in thought and had sauntered off to the garage to work on something.

"I'm going for a walk," Ruby told Aunt Marie after the deputy left.

"By yourself?" Aunt Marie smiled at her. "You could wait till the other girls get back."

Ruby shrugged. "I'm not going far. I'll stay along the lakeshore. I can't get lost."

"Well, I have to make some phone calls," said Aunt

Marie. She sighed, then gave in. "Okay, Ruby. Just, please ... don't wander off."

"I won't," the girl promised. She pulled on her jacket and went out the back door of the lake house. The woods looked so inviting and it would be fun to go walking all alone. Sometimes she had disturbing thoughts about Colorado Springs, and she had to work through those on her own. Doctor Randall had been helpful in some ways, but Ruby hadn't agreed with everything the psychiatrist had suggested for her to do about the trauma in her life.

As she walked, listening to birdsong and catching the quick movement now and then of a chipmunk or a squirrel, Ruby remembered things about long ago, when she had been younger.

When they were small, she and her brother Terry had enjoyed their lives, growing up on Air Force bases because of their dad. Their mom had been lovely and blonde, and seemed to fit right into the lifestyle of having a military husband. The other families on the base had been a close-knit group. Ruby had grown up with plenty of friends her age, and everything had been good in her life until she was about ten.

At that point, their father had increased his duties and was gone most of the time. His assignments took him away from the base and his family, and his wife, Ruth, had not liked it one bit. When he was home, they would argue. Ruby recalled some unpleasant conversations after she'd been sent to bed. Worse, Ruth began drinking heavily and that's when she started to neglect her household chores and often would not even bother to provide meals for herself and her kids. Once in a while there were strangers leaving the house in the mornings.

Terry had tried to protect Ruby as best he could. She also spent more time at her friends' houses, and their parents guessed what was happening and always welcomed her for meals and overnights. Her mother had never been physically abusive toward herself and Terry, but she lived in a dark world known only to herself, and neglect of her children was the result.

It was a blessing that Grandma lived closer to them when the family was stationed in Colorado Springs. Ruby's grandmother was crippled and had a wheelchair, but she provided stability in emotional ways. Although limited in what she was able to do, Grandma helped as much as she could and Ruth permitted it. After Dad was deployed to Vietnam, Grandma fell ill and had to be placed in a nursing home. Then, she had passed away.

So many sad things had occurred in Ruby's young life. When they found out her dad had been shot down and was missing in Vietnam, things really fell apart. Ruth grew worse with her drinking, and Terry tried to shield his sister from their mother's ill behavior. On Thanksgiving she took her own life with sleeping pills, and then the kids had been placed in separate foster homes.

At first, it wasn't so bad, Ruby recalled. She wandered through the woods, keeping the lake in sight the whole time, the events sifting through her mind. There were two other girls about her age living at the Yates' home. Colonel Yates and his wife had a huge home and at first were good to the girls. But it wasn't long before Ruby discovered the Colonel's true nature. He would entice the foster children with candy, presents and little shopping trips and outings. Then, the nightmare … he would demand each girl to undress him. Ruby knew that Mrs. Yates was aware of everything going on, and she never tried to intervene. Ruby had been terrified and when it was her turn to be Colonel Yates' victim, she had put up a fight.

It was only due to Terry's unexpected visit that evening that she had escaped the fate. Looking back now, she could see it without attaching herself to the horror. Doctor Randall had been successful at helping her let go and restore her self-esteem. Thank goodness her brother had shown up when he did. Yet, there had been a violent scene in which Terry had injured Colonel Yates. Thinking he might even have killed the man, Terry took Ruby and they escaped.

Ruby recalled how she and Terry had ridden the Greyhound bus from Denver all the way to Madison, and how they had shown up at Uncle Will's doorstep one morning in December, with snow on the ground and Christmas decorations on the outside of homes in the trailer park. Terry had left the next day, hoping to find out if he had relatives in Wisconsin. He had known that Ruby's father was not his father, yet Ruth had never told her son who his father had been.

Then, after Ruth died, Terry had seen his birth certificate and the name Thomas A. Vetter as his father. Uncle Will had apparently known that Mr. Vetter was dead, and had told Terry, in private, where he might possibly find some relatives. That's when Terry had taken the bus to Black River Falls and then hitch-hiked on a winter's night to Ravensville.

Looking back at last Christmas, Ruby warmed at the memory of riding with Uncle Will up to Ravensville to spend the holiday in a cabin without electricity. Terry had found work on a farm and had planned to spend Christmas in the cabin with them, but then things had intervened. The authorities found out Terry was in the area, and Terry thought he had killed Colonel Yates and that he was wanted for murder.

It had been a miracle last Christmas when Ruby and Terry joined Annette and her mother and became one family in the cozy farmhouse with the woods. Trees had always made Ruby feel secure, and as she looked up at the new spring leaves sprouting, and the beautiful evergreens, she felt happy that she was alive and had a new mom, a new sister, and that Terry was innocent.

However, she still missed her dad very much. She had dreamed about him a lot and had told Doctor Randall about the dreams, but the doctor didn't seem to think they meant much. The dreams had stopped, for the most part. Ruby had been so sure that Dad was alive, yet a couple of months had passed since the last significant dream, and Dad had not come back.

"I know he's still alive," Ruby said out loud to herself. She didn't quite understand why she believed it, except that maybe she loved him so much, she wanted it to be true, even if it wasn't. The others had given up hope. She never would.

Late afternoon shadows reminded her that it was time to turn around and go back to the lake house. Ruby stopped and stared out over the water. Some mallard ducks were bobbing on the waves out a ways from the shore, and across the lake she could make out some distant cottages. The breeze had come up and the air was feeling cooler. She hugged herself and turned to start back.

"Hey, girl," a voice called.

Startled, Ruby glanced around, but didn't see anyone. She started walking again, a little faster.

"Wait a minute," the voice called louder. Suddenly, two older boys stepped out behind some clumps of bushes. One was red-haired with a ruddy complexion, wearing a blue down jacket. The one behind him was taller, dark-haired and wearing a leather jacket with lots of badges on it, with symbols she couldn't see that well. They approached her quickly.

"What do you want?" Ruby asked timidly.

"Are you alone?" asked the red-haired guy.

Ruby gulped and looked around. She knew it wasn't a good idea to let them know she'd come all this way by herself. "N-no ..."

"Liar," accused the tall, dark-haired guy. His piercing dark eyes frightened her and she automatically began walking again, desperately wanting to run, yet afraid that if she did, they'd chase her.

"Where do you live?" the red-haired boy asked.

"Leave me alone," cried Ruby, knowing her voice was trembling. She continued walking, but the boys had caught up to her with their hands in their pockets.

"What's your name?" asked the red-haired boy again.

Ruby didn't answer.

"Hey, girl," taunted the dark-haired one. "I think you're afraid of us. You are, aren't ya?"

The heavier, red-haired boy howled with laughter.

"We have something to show you," said the other one.

"Do you live around here?" asked Red.

Ruby refused to say anything. Instead, she started to run. Her heart was pounding and she sensed she might be in grave danger. What did these two have in mind? Suddenly, the horror of Colonel Yates and that night in Colorado Springs came racing back to her mind and she began to cry.

"Hey, Darrell!" a girl's voice shouted a short distance away. "What are you doing?"

Glancing over her right shoulder, Ruby caught sight of a blonde, curly-haired girl in a brown coat, standing next to the lake. Wasting no more time, Ruby broke into a run and raced toward the lake house. She kept running and did not stop until she saw the rooftop of the garage through the trees. By then, she was breathing so hard, she was gasping and sobbing out of fear.

Ruby slowed, her hand over her chest as her heart continued to pound. She dared to look behind her and saw that no one was chasing her. The girl in the distance had somehow called off the two guys. She sensed they would have molested her, had they gotten hold of her. Now they were nowhere in sight.

She ran at a slower pace all the way back to the lake

house, and as soon as she emerged from the woods, she saw the canoe at the pier, where Fern, Annette and Penny were tying up. Ruby's tears spilled forth and she sobbed as she made her way toward them.

"There's Ruby," called Penny. The other two looked up at her.

"Ruby! What's wrong?" cried Annette.

11

Home Alone

The four girls returned to the lake house. Ruby managed to control her sobs and was able to talk by the time they got to the back patio and sat down. Annette drew her sister up against her on the porch swing. "Tell us," she prompted.

Ruby explained how she had decided to go walking in the woods. "And these two older boys jumped out at me," she said. "They started following me when I turned around."

"Did they try to hurt you?" asked Penny, her green eyes wide with alarm.

"N-no," Ruby admitted, wiping her nose. "But I was afraid they might, so I ran … and they started chasing after me." She paused, then said, "But then this girl called out to them and they quit." She sniffed. "Still, I ran all the way here."

Fern let out a big sigh and shook her head. "That's strange," she commented. "What did the guys look like?"

Ruby told them that one was tall with dark hair and dark eyes, and the other was ruddy complected with red hair. She also told them that the girl had been blonde, but she hadn't gotten a very good look. "She called one of them Darrell," Ruby remembered.

"Do you know them?" Annette asked Fern.

Shaking her head, Fern said, "No. They might have been visitors."

"What about those people Aaron was talking about?" asked Penny. "Do you think …"

"Who's Aaron?" Ruby asked.

Fern signaled to Annette and Penny not to say anything about Aaron in front of Ruby.

"It's not important," Annette said with a smile. "Let's go inside now. Maybe Aunt Marie can make some hot chocolate for us."

It was after dark when Terry got home. He'd left Ginger at the Duncans' and headed straight for the barn to milk Alice, Annette's cow. It had been a hectic, chaotic afternoon in the Duncans' milking parlor. It was always a big hassle when the machinery wasn't working right. Tim and his father, Ray Duncan, were preoccupied with getting repairs made and relieving the poor cows, who were waiting to be milked past their usual time.

When he made his way to the dark farmhouse, he heard the telephone ringing from inside, but by the time he got the door open and turned on the kitchen light, it had stopped ringing. Terry removed his dirty boots and coveralls, then went upstairs to take a shower before fixing himself a sandwich for supper.

As he was drying himself with the towel after stepping out of the shower, he heard the telephone ringing again downstairs. He let it ring. By the time he would have gotten into his pants and climbed down the stairway, he wouldn't have been able to reach the instrument in time as it was located in the dining room downstairs, and the Vetters did not have an extension phone.

Clyde tried to play with Terry. The poor little gray tabby cat was missing the people she was used to having around her, so Terry checked to make sure the cat's dish was full and she had water, then made his supper. It seemed strange to be alone in the house. He had grown so used to having the family around. He missed Ruby and Annette, and he knew that Mom would be back in just a few hours, when her shift ended at the hospital.

Terry had just settled down in the living room with a glass of fresh cow's milk and his tuna sandwich, planning to watch TV, when he heard the phone ring. He popped up off the couch and answered it in the nearby dining room. "Hello?"

"Terry!"

"Debbie!" Terry was elated to hear from Debbie Kelton, one of Annette's school friends, whom he'd been casually dating since February.

"Where've you been?" asked Debbie.

Terry sat in one of the dining room chairs and talked with Debbie for half an hour. They discussed their weekend and chatted about mutual friends and school. Finally, Debbie's father could be heard in the distance on the other end of the line, telling her it was time to hang up.

"Okay, maybe we can get together next Saturday night," Terry suggested. "Think your dad will let you go the movies with me?"

"Sure!" Debbie squealed. "Well, I'd better hang up now. Good night."

"Night, Deb." Terry hung up the phone, then returned to the living room and switched on the program he preferred over the two good channels they got with their antenna. His glass of milk had gotten kind of warm, but he drank it anyway and devoured his sandwich. Then he helped himself to one of Aunt Marie's homemade sweet rolls.

When Mrs. Vetter got home at eleven-thirty that night, Terry had dozed off on the couch with the TV set on. When he heard her, he woke up right away and greeted her, then took his dirty dishes into the kitchen.

"Did anybody call?" asked Mrs. Vetter.

"Just Debbie," said Terry as he headed for the stairs.

"Good night," she called after him.

"Night, Mom."

Mrs. Vetter set her knitting basket and her purse down on the floor and removed her coat. At least Terry was home with her. But she missed Annette and Ruby. And it seemed weird not having Ginger around. As if in answer to her thoughts, Clyde scampered in from the living room and started playing with a stray piece of yarn sticking out of her knitting basket. Mrs. Vetter laughed, then went to the stove to make herself a cup of tea before going up to bed.

"In another five years, the kids'll leave home," she said to herself, reaching into the cupboard. "Then I'm going to be here all alone." She sighed. "Hmm … what will that be like?" Then she stared out the kitchen window into the dark of night and thought about Earl.

Annette slept well that night at the lake house. When Monday morning dawned, she was wide awake, being used to getting up early to milk her cows. Penny and Ruby were still sleeping soundly as she got up, stretched, and looked out the window over the lake. Light reflected over the body of water and the sky was in various shades of pink, lavender and light blue with trees silhouetted along the edges.

It was chilly, but she resisted burrowing back into bed beside Penny. Instead, she noiselessly picked out some clothes and carried them out of the bedroom, down the hall to the bathroom. Then she quietly went downstairs to get a glass of juice from the kitchen and carried it into the big room to sit in front of the large stone fireplace, which was still burning some coals from the night before. There was a small stack of firewood in a wooden box next to her, so she put her glass of juice down and opened the fireplace doors to insert some sticks and build up the fire. She wondered what they were going to do today. The Parkers had suggested a visit to a museum in town and seeing some of the sights the area had to offer.

Annette sat back in one of the big comfortable chairs to watch the logs catch fire. She thought about the boy, Aaron, who was staying at the shack across the lake. She knew Fern wasn't telling her everything. Aaron had seemed nice enough. She didn't totally agree that he was doing the right thing by avoiding the draft by hiding out in the North Woods. Yet she could understand why someone would rebel at being forced to go into service if they didn't want to.

She thought of Tim again. She knew Tim would never burn his draft card. She wasn't even sure he had one yet. The very notion of Tim Duncan getting drafted and going to Vietnam scared her so much … and the same with her brother Terry. Because Tim had gotten into the university, he would be deferred. Annette hoped and prayed that by the time her brother turned eighteen, the stupid war would be over. Poor Ruby's father had vanished with little hope of him ever being found. It had to be absolute agony for his family.

By the time Annette had gotten the fire going again and her juice glass was empty, she heard someone moving around in the back of the lake house. She wandered into the kitchen to find Aunt Marie brewing a pot of coffee. "Oh, good morning, Nettie," she said.

Annette cringed, but let it go. "Good morning."

"Sleep okay?"

"Yes, just fine," said Annette.

"You're certainly up early," said Aunt Marie as she started heating the percolator.

"I can't help it," said Annette. "I guess I'm used to it."

Aunt Marie smiled and motioned for Annette to sit down at the counter with her. "Do you like living out in the country?"

Annette nodded.

"And now you've got a brother and a sister."

"Terry and Ruby are great," said Annette.

"Your mom seems happy," commented Aunt Marie.

"I think she is," said Annette.

"You sound a little dubious," said her aunt.

Annette grimaced. "Well ... at least she's a lot happier than she was before Christmas."

"How do you mean?"

Annette looked at her aunt and hesitated. "Maybe I shouldn't tell you this."

"You can tell me anything, Nettie."

Annette sighed and studied her fingernails. "Sometimes I think my mom gets lonely." When her aunt did not comment, Annette explained. "In November she was dating this man named Earl Warner. She met him at the hospital, when he was a patient."

"Yes," said Aunt Marie, "I remember Helen mentioning him. What happened to him?"

"She didn't tell you?" Annette was incredulous.

"No."

Annette sighed, then said, "Earl had asked her to marry him. He was going to provide for us, but we were going to have to move to Black River Falls."

"And she turned him down?" asked her aunt.

"Not exactly," said Annette and swallowed. "I kind of talked my mom out of it." She hung her head. "Maybe I shouldn't have made such a big deal over it, because I know Mom really liked him. I don't think she's gotten over him."

"You didn't like this man?"

Annette had to tell her aunt all of it. "Earl Warner proposed to my mother under false pretenses. He's a land developer, and he came to Ravensville to buy up farm land and turn it all into recreational property."

"Well, what's wrong with that?" asked Aunt Marie. "It's our bread and butter here on the lake."

"Yes, but Minocqua is a resort town," said Annette. "Ravensville would have been ruined without all the little farms that operate there. It would have put a lot of people out of business … maybe even the Duncans. And … and he would have bought our forty acres and turned it into hunting lodges!"

"Well, I see your point," said Aunt Marie. She placed her hand on Annette's wrist. "I think you are a wise young lady, Annette. You've grown up so much in the last couple of years."

"I don't think Mom's interested in seeing any other men after Earl," Annette added. "But she's lived all these years without a husband. Of course she was busy working and raising *me*. And now she's got Terry and Ruby as well. Still, sometimes I think she gets a bit lonely."

Footsteps approached from the back door to the kitchen and Uncle Joe stepped inside. He grinned when he saw Annette. "Good morning, ladies."

"Good morning, Uncle Joe," said Annette.

"That coffee ready yet, woman?" he asked his wife.

"It's perking," said Aunt Marie. She got up from the counter and walked to the large refrigerator. "I'll get out those hot cross buns and warm them up for everybody."

Uncle Joe rubbed his hands together. "Where are the kids? Still sleeping?"

"It's spring break," Aunt Marie reminded him.

"What about you?" Uncle Joe stared at Annette. "Why aren't you sleeping late?"

"Nettie's a dairy farmer," quipped Aunt Marie and shot a wink at her niece.

12

The Ojibwe Museum

B ob checked out of his motel room later that morning, then stopped for coffee and an order of toast at a local café. He sat at the counter and pondered what he should do next in his search for Ruby and Terry.

"More coffee?" The friendly brunette waitress hovered over him with her coffee pot and he nodded his head.

"Do you know of a place called The Lake House?" Bob asked the waitress, whose nametag read "Betty."

The woman filled his cup, then winced. "The Lake House? Which one? There are probably half a dozen or more lodges with that name in Minocqua," she told him.

This was not what Bob wanted to hear. He scratched his head and frowned. "Oh boy ..."

"Do you know the name of the people who run it?" the waitress asked.

Bob shook his head. "No."

"Do you even know which lake it's on?" Betty stared at him, holding the pot of coffee in one hand.

Bob sighed, then took a sip of his warmed up coffee.

"You know, you might stop by the Chamber of Commerce," Betty suggested. "They should have a list of all the resorts in the area."

Bob got directions to the Chamber office, thanked the waitress, then drank up his coffee. He left a one-dollar bill on the counter, then got up and walked out the door. The Chamber of Commerce was just up the street. He hoped they were open today.

At seven o'clock Terry had gotten up to milk Annette's cow, grabbed a bite of breakfast, and had left to go to work at the Randt farm.

An hour had passed by the time Mrs. Vetter got out of bed. She still wore her bathrobe and trudged downstairs, feeling a little groggy. She hadn't had a decent night's sleep. She could see that Terry had fed Ginger and filled the cat's dish. She also found his note on the kitchen table that said he'd taken care of the cows and would be home by six.

Mrs. Vetter made a pot of coffee and set it on the stove to percolate. The house seemed emptier than usual with the kids gone. How quickly she had gotten used to their presence and the uplifting sound of voices and laughter when they were there.

After the coffee was ready, she popped two slices of bread into the toaster, then got the butter dish out of the refrigerator. Looking outside the window over the sink, she saw that it was going to be a cloudy day. At least they'd had a beautiful weekend for Easter.

When the telephone rang, Mrs. Vetter went into the dining room to answer it. She was surprised to hear Tim Duncan's voice. "Good morning, Helen."

"Well, good morning, Tim," she said. "Is everything all right? Terry told me about the milking machine going down. Is it up and running today?"

"Yes, everything's okay now," said Tim. "Say, is Terry around?"

"Why no, Tim. He's working over at the Randts' today, helping them build the new fence around the pastures."

"Yeah, that's right," Tim remembered. "Well, you'll want to know this as well."

Mrs. Vetter heard the toast pop up and interrupted him. "Tim, hang on. My toast just popped up." She set the receiver down and hurried back into the kitchen to quickly butter her toast. Then she returned to the dining room. "Sorry, Tim," she said after picking up the receiver.

"I thought you'd like to know that yesterday morning a man came to your house," Tim said.

Her first thought was Earl, and she felt her heart quicken. Earl Warner, however, had not contacted her since the end of November. "Who was it?" she asked.

"Well, he was asking for Terry and Ruby."

"Good heavens," said Mrs. Vetter. "I hope this doesn't mean trouble from Social Services. Why, I can't imagine what ..."

"No, Helen," Tim cut in. "You won't believe this, but he said his name was Bob Foley."

After a short pause, Mrs. Vetter let out a loud gasp. "Oh Tim ... are you sure?"

"He said he was their father." Tim hesitated, then added, "I'd completely spaced out telling Terry about it yesterday because of our emergency with the milking machine. I tried calling Terry a couple of times last night, but he didn't answer the phone, and then it was busy."

"Tim, what did Bob say?" asked Mrs. Vetter.

Tim explained how he'd told Bob Foley that the family had driven to Minocqua for spring break. He didn't have the phone number of the lake house, nor did he remember the last name of Mrs. Vetter's sister and her husband.

"Then what did he do?" asked Mrs. Vetter.

"He left," said Tim.

"My word!" Mrs. Vetter pulled a dining room chair out from the table and sat down. "Well, did he say where he might be staying?"

Tim told her that Bob had said he was going to find the lake house and his kids.

"He's … alive," murmured Mrs. Vetter in amazement. "Ruby's father is alive."

"Yes," said Tim. "He also said that Uncle Will in Madison gave him your address. Uncle Will was supposed to call you and let you know that he was coming."

"Only nobody was home," said Mrs. Vetter. "Tim, thank you. I'm going to hang up now and I'll call Will right away."

Flustered, Mrs. Vetter allowed herself a couple of minutes to finish her coffee and eat her toast. Then, with trembling fingers, she dialed the long distance number of Will Knutson in Madison. The other end rang and rang. She hung up after she realized Will had probably left for work. Then she sighed.

"Terry needs to know as soon as possible," Mrs. Vetter said out loud. She decided to get dressed and drive right over to the Randt farm to find him. Halfway up the stairs, she stopped and turned around, then came back down. Then she dialed the number at the lake house.

No one answered at the lake house because Uncle Joe and Aunt Marie had taken the four girls to town for some sightseeing. First they went to the Historical Museum and saw exhibits about logging in the olden days, along with fishing and maple syrup. They spent an hour and a half in the Ojibwe Museum, and Uncle Joe shared his knowledge of the Ojibwe Tribe, taking pride in his ancestral heritage.

"*You're* an Indian?" Ruby had asked Uncle Joe in astonishment in the car on the way over.

Both Uncle Joe and Aunt Marie had laughed.

"My dad is one-fourth Native American," explained Fern.

Annette, of course, had known that he was, and Fern also exhibited the darker complexion and brown eyes of her father's heritage.

The museum had a re-created Ojibwe village, which they toured as well. The Ojibwe people had built dome-shaped wigwams out of poles that were lashed together. Then they would cover them with woven mats and bark from birch trees.

"Gosh, I didn't know that the name Wisconsin came from an Ojibwe name," Penny remarked after they came out of the museum.

"That's right, Penny," said Uncle Joe. "It actually was derived from the name of the Wisconsin River—*Wishkonsing*."

"Interesting," said Penny. "And I learned there are over a hundred and twenty-five bands of Ojibwe people living in Canada."

"Which isn't that far away, actually," said Annette.

"What does Ojibwe mean?" asked Ruby.

"This may sound kind of silly to you," said Uncle Joe, putting his arm around the girl's shoulders as they walked back to the car, "but Ojibwe means 'puckered up.'"

Ruby scrunched up her face and looked at him. "Why would they be called that?"

Fern giggled. "It's probably because the Ojibwe wore their moccasins with a puckered seam on the toe. Right, Dad?"

Uncle Joe nodded. "Or maybe it was because they were good kissers." He squeezed his mouth together and made kissing sounds, which caused an eruption of more laughter.

"Oh, Joe, stop!" chuckled Aunt Marie. "Is anyone hungry for lunch?"

Several "yeses" responded.

"Can we eat at Paul Bunyan's?" asked Fern.

"The lumberjack?" Annette asked.

"It's the name of one of our favorite restaurants in Minocqua," said Aunt Marie.

"I could use a hamburger," said Ruby boldly.

"Well, then burgers and fries it is," said Uncle Joe and picked up the pace as they all hurried to the parked car.

Mrs. Vetter drove her car over to the Randt farm as soon as she was dressed. Terry was with Pete and his dad and brother Mark, working out in the fields. Marge Randt sent Kay, her 12-year-old daughter, out to tell Terry his mother needed to talk to him.

"Laura is certainly growing fast," remarked Mrs. Vetter. The baby was sitting on a blanket on the floor of the living room, surrounded by toys and an adoring bunch of Randt siblings. "And she is a real beauty with that dark curly hair."

Marge Randt carried in two cups of hot tea she had just made in the kitchen. She handed one to Mrs. Vetter. "Yes, Laura is a little over four months old now. She has settled down into a much better sleep pattern."

"And how are *you* feeling?" Mrs. Vetter knew that Mrs. Randt had experienced complications during the birth of her ninth child and couldn't have any more children.

"Oh, I'm slowly getting back to normal." Marge stirred a spoon of sugar into her tea.

"How is the farm coming along?" Mrs. Vetter dunked her teabag a couple of times. She knew that the Randts were struggling just to make ends meet, and she was still amazed that Earl Warner had tried to buy their property to turn it into a hunting lodge.

"Things are so-so," Marge revealed. "I think that with Terry's help, Ron is not so discouraged. He wishes he could pay him more."

"Terry understands." Mrs. Vetter patted the other woman's hand.

"So, your girls are up north," commented Marge in an effort to change the subject.

"Yes. And I miss them."

They chatted a little longer, and Mrs. Vetter's tea was almost gone when Kay showed up at the door with Terry. When he entered and saw his mother, he looked very worried.

"Is anything wrong? Are Annette and Ruby okay?" he asked as he removed his muddy shoes at the door.

Mrs. Vetter stood up. "They're fine," she reassured him. "But I've got some news." She shot a glance at Mrs. Randt, who immediately took the hint and got up from the table.

"You can talk in the kitchen," she said, shooing the rest of her children into the other room.

Terry followed Mrs. Vetter into the kitchen and he stared at her, still worried. "Mom, what's happened?"

"Terry ... it's your dad ..."

He shook his head in confusion, and Mrs. Vetter immediately corrected her error.

"I mean ... Ruby's dad ... Bob."

"Huh?"

"Terry, Tim said Bob came to the house yesterday morning, while we were up in Minocqua. He was looking for you and Ruby."

"Bob's *alive?*" Terry's blue eyes almost bulged out. "Is he here?"

She quickly explained to him what Tim had told her, how he had left for Minocqua.

"But ... why didn't Tim tell me?" Terry looked confused.

"He tried to call last night," explained Mrs. Vetter. "He said he was so preoccupied with the milking machine breaking down yesterday that he forgot to inform you."

Terry appeared angry for a moment. "What?" Then he sighed and said, "Never mind. What are we gonna do, Mom?"

"I don't know. I tried calling the lake house before I came over here. Apparently they've all gone somewhere."

"How did he know to come to Ravensville?"

"I guess Will gave him our address," said Mrs. Vetter. "I tried calling Uncle Will too, but he wasn't home. He may have tried to get hold of us to let us know Bob was coming. At least that's what Tim told me."

"Mom … Ruby is going to freak out."

"Well, apparently Ruby has been right all along." She managed a smile.

"Do you have to work tonight?" Terry knew his mother had to work, but what he meant was *did* she have to go in, or could they drive back up to the lake house?

13

Conscientious Objector

B ob left the Chamber of Commerce with a list of all the lodging houses in the area, which was extensive. After viewing the big map on the wall with all the surrounding lakes, he came to understand why Minocqua was called "the island city."

He had no idea how he was going to find the lake house where Ruby and Terry were staying. His funds were dwindling and he couldn't afford a motel every night. He figured he could find a campground or two, where he might be able to sleep in his Ford Falcon, but it certainly would not be too comfortable. Besides, being early April in northern Wisconsin, the nights were still frigid.

"I'll call Will," he said after he got into his car and got the engine started. "I'll find out if he talked to that woman." There was a phone booth on the corner by the drugstore, so he parked outside and slipped inside, pulling out the scrap of paper with Will's phone number.

Will didn't answer, which came as no surprise. Bob figured his brother-in-law was still at work. With a sigh, he recovered his coins, dropped them in his pants pocket, and walked back to his car. Then he decided to drive out to the big lake and just cruise around. He really didn't know what else to do and was feeling more depressed as the day wore on.

E veryone was tired later that afternoon after they returned to the lake house. They had seen a lot of the tourist stops in town and were so full of burgers, fries and milkshakes that Aunt Marie said she wouldn't be cooking a big supper that night.

"Wanna go out in the canoe again?" Fern asked the girls.

Annette and Penny glanced at each other and smiled. They both knew that Fern wanted to go check on Aaron across the lake.

"*I* want to go this time," cried Ruby, who was plopped on the floor, petting Jabbo in front of the fireplace. "Is there room in the canoe for four?"

"Sure," said Annette, then looked at Fern to see if she thought it was all right.

"You can come," said Fern.

Soon they were dressed warmly, since the sun was hiding behind clouds that day and the wind had increased a bit. Penny offered to paddle with Fern this time, to give Annette a break.

Ruby loved riding in the canoe and chattered about everything she saw. Annette and Penny commented every now and then, but Annette noticed Fern was really quiet.

"I wish *we* had a boat," said Ruby, running her hand through the water outside the canoe as it moved forward.

"Tim has a little rubber raft," said Penny.

"Yeah, sometimes we use it on Duncan's pond in early summer," Annette explained.

"A canoe would be too big for our pond," chuckled Penny. "But it's a great swimming hole."

"And you can skate on it in the winter," Annette added.

"Do you miss your brother?" Ruby asked Fern.

Startled, Fern glanced up at Ruby, then smiled. "David? Yeah, I guess."

"When will he be coming home from the war?" Ruby asked.

"I don't know," said Fern. "Mom and Dad think sometime in August, when his tour will be up." Then she added, "That is, if he survives."

Everyone was silent. Ruby hung her head, suddenly reminded that her father was still in Vietnam and, in fact, may not have survived.

"Look, I see a heron." Annette pointed off toward the swamp to the left.

"Oh, can you get closer?" Ruby perked up. "I've never seen a heron."

"Sure," said Fern, and started turning the canoe in that direction.

Annette kept her eyes on the long-legged bird that was perched on a fallen log on the shoreline. It was too small to be a great blue, she decided. But she couldn't tell if it was a little green heron or something else.

Within five minutes the canoe was gliding through the weedy waters of the swamp and they slowed, watching the shorebird, which stood very still as it watched them approach.

"Oh, it's so pretty," said Penny.

Suddenly, a shot rang out and the blast echoed through the atmosphere. The girls jumped and the heron flapped its long wings and took to flight, heading to their right.

"Stay quiet!" Fern commanded in a hushed voice. "And don't move."

Their eyes wide with fear, the girls did as Fern said, waiting breathlessly to see if the person who'd fired a gun would come into sight. She kept the canoe steady in the water, not wanting to draw attention to themselves. She hoped that the weeds hid them from view.

Annette's heart was beating fast as she reached for her little sister and held her close. Ruby was trembling and Penny was bent over in the canoe, cowering. After a minute of silence, Fern signaled that they could start paddling again, but then loud voices came from the woods.

A young woman's voice rang out, "You idiots! What do you think you're doing?"

Then they heard a young man reply sarcastically, "Lay off, Brenda. We're just having a little fun."

"You'll draw attention to yourselves," she chided from behind some nearby trees. "That's the last thing we need."

"Who died and made *you* boss?" whined a deeper voice, and then Annette could see a boy about college age, standing in the trees. He had dark hair and was wearing a leather jacket.

"We were just having some fun," said another young man, who was hidden from view. "Come on, Brenda ..."

"Nick, do you want someone to call the sheriff?" the girl demanded.

"Knock it off, Darrell." The other boy came into sight and had red hair. "We might need that .22 you got off that old man on the fishing boat. He didn't leave us a lot of ammo."

"Let's go," called Brenda, her voice trailing off as she moved further into the woods. "There's an unlocked cabin I discovered this morning ..."

When the dark-haired guy walked into the woods, the girls knew the trio was leaving, so they turned the canoe around and started paddling quickly and silently back into the middle of the lake. Fern steered it toward the shore where Aaron was staying in his shack.

"That was scary!" said Ruby.

"We could have been shot," added Penny, her green eyes still wide as she paddled frantically.

"Those were the people that chased me yesterday," Ruby told them. "I recognized their voices."

"I think we should report them to the sheriff," said Annette.

"Yeah, it sounded like they wanted to ransack somebody's cabin or something," said Penny, breathing hard from the labor.

Fern glanced at the others and said, "We'll tell somebody as soon as we get home. But first … I need to check on Aaron. Make sure he's all right."

"Who's Aaron?" Ruby asked again.

Fern didn't respond, so Annette told Ruby, "He's this guy staying in one of the cottages."

"You can't tell Aunt Marie or Uncle Joe," warned Penny.

"Oh," said Ruby. "It's a secret?"

"Kind of," said Annette.

"Just for now." Fern gave Ruby a smile of reassurance, then let the canoe drift a little as they were approaching the bank.

"Promise not to say anything?" asked Annette.

"I promise." Ruby smiled.

Aaron invited them inside his place when they arrived several minutes later. Everyone was cold from being on the lake, and Aaron had a little fire going in his antique wood stove in the barren living room of the cottage.

The place definitely had been abandoned, and Aaron was doing his best to make it habitable, though Annette wondered how he'd managed over the winter with those broken windows. He had set up some crates for furniture and he used tree stumps for seats. In the corner she saw he had fixed up a sleeping bag with blankets and had a little shelf with some magazines and a candle.

"Aaron's only been here since early March," Fern explained. "We met when he was fishing on the bank and I came by in the canoe."

Looking around, Annette saw that Aaron had a few staples to live on, such as a loaf of bread, a jar of peanut butter, some oranges and a bag of potatoes. She learned that Fern often sneaked food from her parents' lodge to take to him. He was always grateful for whatever food he could find, and he had set some snares in the woods and cooked himself a rabbit or two.

Fern told Aaron about the shots being fired in the swamp and how they had overheard the three young people in the woods.

"They are trouble makers," Aaron insisted. His expression had turned to one of rage. "They have been raiding people's cabins and vandalizing, and they're proud of it!"

Annette told about Ruby's encounter with the vagabonds the afternoon before, when she'd gone for a walk in the woods.

"Did you tell your parents?" Aaron asked Fern.

"No."

"You need to," he told her. "I don't want to see anyone getting hurt. And if they have a gun ..."

"It sounds like they got the rifle from Leroy," said Fern. "We overheard them talking about getting the gun from the old fisherman in the swamp. That had to be Leroy."

"What do you suppose happened?" Penny was alarmed.

"Do you think they caused his death?" asked Annette.

"I'm not sure the sheriff's department looked into it that much," said Fern. "I heard Daddy say Leroy collapsed when he was standing up in the boat, and they think it must have been his heart."

"Well, I wouldn't put it past those freaks!" Aaron was still livid. "They tried to rough *me* up."

"They haven't been back, have they?" asked Fern.

"There's nothing here for them to steal," said Aaron, "but don't worry, Fern. I'm watching my back." He pulled her closer to him and smiled.

"Ooh, that fire sure feels good," said Penny, unzipping her jacket.

"We really should be getting back to the lake house soon," said Fern. She had already unloaded some fruit and cookies from her knapsack for Aaron.

"What are you doing here, anyway?" Ruby asked Aaron.

"Ruby ..." Annette tried to silence her sister.

"I mean, are you hiding out or something?"

Aaron looked befuddled and Fern rolled her eyes. "Ruby, Aaron's got nowhere else to go," she explained.

"Well then, why doesn't he go stay at the lake house? You've got lots of room there."

Penny sighed. "Fern's dad wouldn't like that," she said.

Fern nodded and smiled at Ruby. "It's kind of a long story."

"Did you do something wrong?" Ruby wasn't about to give it up.

Annette cleared her throat. "It's getting late. Maybe we should ..."

"I'm a conscientious objector," Aaron admitted, looking Ruby right in the eye.

"What's that?" asked the girl.

"I don't believe in war," said Aaron.

"Oh." Ruby didn't know what to say.

"They were trying to make me go to Vietnam," he explained in a calm voice. "I refused. And I had to run away ... or they'd arrest me and put me in jail, then make me go anyway."

"Oh." Ruby blinked her eyes, thinking hard about what he'd said.

"War is a terrible thing," Aaron continued in a calm voice. "And it is senseless."

Ruby nodded her head. "I know what you say is true," she said. "And maybe Vietnam is a waste. That's what people say anyway." Her eyelids fluttered as she stared at the floor. "My dad ... my dad's Missing in Action ... he's in Vietnam ... he might be *dead*." Her voice trembled as she looked at Aaron's face and tears began to seep from her blue eyes.

"Oh, Ruby." Annette reached over and gave her a hug.

Aaron stood up and walked to the back of the room, his hands in his pockets. "You'd better go before it starts getting dark," he told the girls.

Fern rose and went over to console Aaron, but he brushed her gently away. Then she led Annette, Penny and Ruby outside, where the wind had picked up and it looked like a storm might be brewing. "We'd better get back to the lake house."

"Yikes," said Penny.

As soon as they were in the canoe, Penny and Fern paddled while Annette sat beside Ruby, who continued to sniffle as they headed across the huge body of water to the other side. With any luck, they'd make it before the rain fell.

14

Cold Night on the Lake

Unsuccessful in finding the lake house he was searching for, Bob purchased a can of Spam and some Beanie-Weanies at the small grocery store outside of town. Then he drove partly around the big lake, looking for a suitable place to park—some wooded area that was out of the way. He'd decided to spend the night camping and planned to sleep in the back seat of the Falcon.

A storm was moving into the area, he noticed, as he built a small campfire beside the lake. The waves were building and the wind made it difficult for him to get the fire started, but he finally managed. Next, he opened the food cans with his little Army can opener and placed the food next to the fire to heat it. He was glad he'd brought his heavy jacket along, which had a hood he could pull over his head. He rubbed his hands together as the flames danced and grew, consuming the pieces of dry wood he'd collected around him.

He smiled as he stared at the can of Spam as carbon from the flames turned the metal black. He used to dislike the stuff. But in Vietnam, troops regarded Spam as a prized possession, as well as Beanie-Weanies. He had developed an appetite for it, especially after not having anything to eat when he and Bill

Crawford, his pilot, had been shot down and had wandered through the jungles, dodging the Viet Cong.

Bob's memory was sporadic, but more and more he was starting to piece things together. He knew that his involvement in secret missions like Operation Ground Hog had meant taking risks. He had been trained to survive, and he had chosen to work undercover at times.

After his ordeal, he knew his career was over. Yet he'd been told that someone would contact him from time to time, to see what other information might surface from his failing memory. Physically, he wasn't sure he could work again … at anything. But the doctors had advised him to just take his time. He still needed to heal from his wounds, as well as the trauma he'd undergone.

"Now I'm home," Bob muttered to himself. "I've come home to a family that no longer exists." Ruth was gone, and Will had told him Mrs. Vetter—Tom Vetter's widow—was planning to legally adopt Terry and Ruby. Where did that leave him? How would Ruby feel now, seeing him the way he was—with a flawed body and mind?

Perhaps it was best just to leave the kids alone, let them live their lives. Will had said they were happy living in Ravensville. He didn't want to take that happiness away from them. Why shake things up? Hadn't it been traumatic enough for that sweet daughter of his?

"Life sure isn't fair," Bob said with a sigh.

It was five-thirty that afternoon when Mrs. Vetter and Terry arrived at the lake house. It had started to rain and the wind blew, causing tall evergreens in the front yard to sway. Three hours ago, after they had dropped Ginger off at the Duncans' farm, Terry talked to Tim and his dad.

Tim had agreed to tend to Annette's cows again, but Ray Duncan was concerned about the work load without Terry helping them out. Terry promised to return as soon as possible. They wished Mrs. Vetter and Terry luck in finding his stepdad.

Mr. Randt had also understood and gave Terry as much time off as he needed. As for the hospital, Mrs. Vetter felt her children mattered more than her job. She didn't like putting pressure on the nurses on her floor, yet most of them, she knew, understood. She had worked with her crew for several years, and when she called in, the head nurse agreed to her time off.

"Helen, what are you doing here?" cried Aunt Marie when they entered the lake house. She and Uncle Joe were going over some ledgers behind the reception desk.

"I tried calling earlier today," explained Mrs. Vetter, "but there was no answer."

"Is anything wrong?" asked Uncle Joe.

"Where's Ruby?" Terry asked, looking around.

"Why, Fern took the girls out on the lake after we got home from town," said Aunt Marie. "I'm surprised they're not back yet."

"It's pretty stormy out there," said Terry. "Are they out in the canoe?"

Peeking out a window curtain, Uncle Joe blinked in surprise. "It's raining."

Aunt Marie stepped out from behind the counter and gave her sister a quick hug. "Helen, what's happened? You look worried."

Uncle Joe came and stood beside his wife as Mrs. Vetter explained about Ruby's father stopping by the farm while they were gone. "And our neighbor boy thinks he was headed here to Minocqua. He is looking for Ruby and Terry."

"I'm going out to the pier," said Uncle Joe and grabbed his jacket off a hook on the wall.

"Oh dear," said Aunt Marie. "But … but I thought Ruby's father was …"

"We're rather surprised as well," said Mrs. Vetter.

"Did your neighbor tell this man to come here?" asked Aunt Marie.

"No, that's the thing," said Terry. "Tim couldn't remember your name, and he didn't have the phone number."

"Our mistake," grumbled Mrs. Vetter.

"Maybe we should contact the authorities," suggested Aunt Marie. "You know, the police? Do you know what he was driving?"

Terry shook his head. "I never thought to ask Tim."

Aunt Marie nodded, then went behind the counter again and began paging through a notebook. "My guess is, he might be staying at one of the other lodges or even in a motel."

They heard the door close as Uncle Joe left the lake house. Terry touched Mrs. Vetter's arm and said, "I'm going with Uncle Joe." Then he ran outside.

"If that's the case, Marie, then it's like looking for a needle in a haystack. There are too many places where he could be right now."

"True," said Aunt Marie, "but I've got an idea."

The girls had left Aaron's shack half an hour before, but the lake had become so rough and choppy, they grew frightened. Even Fern, who was an expert at small craft navigation, had all but panicked. When Ruby saw the rocking waves and felt the cold wind in her face, she had started to cry. Annette and Ruby huddled together while Penny struggled to hold onto her paddle.

"We're going to have to get to shore," Fern shouted over the wind and rain. "We can't possibly get back across the lake right now."

"Can we go back to Aaron's?" Penny's teeth chattered from the chill.

"No, I think we should head for the nearest land," Fern

decided. "This way ..."

The canoe pitched and the girls screamed as the waves climbed around them. Fern commanded Penny to keep paddling, and Annette wrapped her arms tightly around her little sister. "Hang on, Ruby," she said, "we're gonna make it."

"I'm so scared!" cried the younger girl.

"I know. Me too." Annette thought of her mom and Terry, of Tim and Ginger ... all those she loved. The good thing was they all had their life jackets on. But she knew the lake was very cold and they could die of hypothermia if they did not get to land soon and find shelter from this storm.

Having finished his G.I. supper, Bob sat by his campfire for several more minutes, then decided to get some shut-eye. He could tell it would be dark soon, so he might as well just call it a day and crawl into the back seat of the Falcon. He had certainly been through much worse. He stomped out his fire, then took a short stroll into the woods before returning to the car.

It was barely twilight and he had slipped off to sleep, his blanket wrapped around him, when he heard voices outside the car. Bob immediately woke up, but did not move. The voices came closer.

"Look at this old beater," said a young man with a deep voice. "What a wreck."

Another boy laughed. Bob could tell they were closing in on him. He did not move.

"Hey, it doesn't even have plates."

"There's a temp in the back window," the first young man said. "See?" A flashlight beam streaked over the car as Bob waited to see what they would do next.

"What's that read? Colorado? Hey, I think it says Colorado, Darrell."

"Let's see if there's anything good inside," said the deeper voice.

"Nick! Darrell!" a girl's voice called from a short distance. "Come on ... the coast is clear."

"Oops, there's Brenda," said the boy.

"Hurry up!" she called in an impatient voice. "They could come home at any minute. I need help with the stash."

The flashlight beam disappeared and Bob waited till they'd left. He slowly sat up in the back seat and looked out the windows. He couldn't see very much in the dark, but off to his left, he saw the flashlight beam bobbing on the ground. The three young people had avoided discovering him. "They're lucky," he chuckled as he snuggled back underneath his blanket. "Or I might have had to introduce them to Mama Ruger ..."

The girls had managed to reach shore near the swamp. They were all wet and cold from the rain. Ruby was shivering as they dragged the canoe up out of the water. They'd had to wade through part of the swamp to get to the bank. Darkness was coming fast now, but there was still a little bit of daylight to see. Fern had remembered to carry a penlight in her knapsack, which was wet from the water that had gotten into the canoe. But it still worked.

"How are we gonna get back to the lake house?" fretted Penny, hugging herself.

"I don't know," said Fern. "No telling how long it will take to walk around the lake, plus we'd have to leave the canoe here."

Annette looked around, but all she could see were woods as the wind continued to blow through the trees and cold rain pattered down on them. "Well, we need to get warm somehow," she told the others.

"How far are we from Aaron's place?" asked Penny.

"I'm not sure," confessed Fern, "but I think we're quite a ways."

"Maybe we're close to a road," suggested Annette, her lip trembling from the chill.

"I think there is a road," agreed Fern. "Come on, let's walk a ways and see."

"But we can't see in the dark," called Penny in protest. "And what if there are ... bears?"

At the mention of bears, Ruby let out a shriek and clung to Annette.

"There are no bears," Annette chided, then turned to her cousin. "Are there?"

Fern didn't answer. "Come on, let's get started," she said. "Stay close to each other. There's still just a bit of daylight left. At least we can find some place that's a little drier."

"Don't you have a brighter flashlight or something in that knapsack?" asked Penny.

"All I have is this penlight," said Fern, "but I'm not sure how long it will last. It needs a new battery."

Penny followed Annette, who held onto Ruby, as Fern led the way slowly through the dark evergreens. As they got under the trees, the rain didn't reach them as much, but it was getting harder to see, and often they would stumble on rocks or logs or bushes.

"Are they back?" Mrs. Vetter drew the kitchen curtain aside and looked outside as she saw a couple of moving flashlight beams near the shore.

"I sure hope so," said Aunt Marie. She went to the door and opened it, then called out into the dark, "Joe!"

A moment later, Uncle Joe and Terry came into the house, their hair wet from the rain. "No sign of them," he reported, turning off his flashlight. Terry did the same.

"Joe, I'm worried," Aunt Marie exclaimed. "They should have been back here an hour ago."

"Where did they go?" asked Mrs. Vetter.

"Fern knows the lake really well," Aunt Marie reassured her sister. "Maybe when they saw it was going to storm, they paddled to shore to wait it out."

"Only now it's dark," said Terry. "How are they going to return in the dark?"

"Let's not panic," said Uncle Joe, looking out the window. He sighed. "I think it's time we called the Coast Guard."

Mrs. Vetter looked alarm, and Terry wrinkled up his face and said, "What? Are you serious?"

Aunt Marie rolled her eyes. "He means the local constabulary." She shook her head as she led them out into the lobby. "I'm going to call the sheriff."

B ob had not been able to sleep. He was worried that he might get another visit from those vagabonds who had almost discovered him. He sensed they were up to no good. But on the other hand, he didn't want to get involved in local crime. No doubt they were just some local kids up to some spring break mischief, though he didn't like the idea of them breaking into people's cabins.

After a few minutes, he sat up and decided to revive his campfire. He had some water in his thermos and a stash of instant coffee. The rain seemed to have let up and the air was frigid after the storm. He climbed out of the Falcon and bundled his jacket around himself, then walked around in search of some dry sticks. There were some pieces of wood underneath his car that had not gotten wet, and he got down on his knees and collected enough to get his fire going.

A loon called from somewhere on the lake as he blew on the tiny flame to build it up. What a lonely, eerie sound that was. He had to admit, though … the North Woods of Wisconsin was quite an experience. There was beauty and clean air. It sure beat those sweltering jungles he had suffered in for so long.

From what he'd seen of Wisconsin so far, he liked it here. He wondered how Ruby and Terry felt about being in the Midwest after all the different places they'd lived because of his military career.

Half an hour passed. Bob fixed his instant coffee and was sipping the hot, aromatic beverage out of his tin cup as he sat on a wet log in front of his fire. He was aware of footsteps and immediately grew alert. His right hand slowly reached for the cloth camo bag he had leaning against a rock beside him. He wanted to be sure his Ruger was ready, in case he needed it.

Then a voice behind him said, "Hello. Mind if I join you?"

Carefully, Bob turned toward the sound, one hand holding his coffee cup, the other on the butt of his revolver. He couldn't see who it was, but it was the voice of a male. "Identify yourself," he said in a calm voice. "And don't move."

The person was standing just six feet away, yet Bob could not see him in the dark, though he knew his own face was visible from the fire light. There was a loud sigh and then a young man spoke. "My name's Aaron. I mean you no harm."

"Come closer," said Bob, holding his position.

The young man stepped forward, careful not to cause this stranger, in his eyes, to react. Bob could see a tall, lanky college-age boy with long, scraggly hair and glasses, wearing an overcoat. "I saw your fire," he said with a tremble in his voice. "Then I saw your car. Are you camping?" Aaron knelt beside Bob and started rubbing his hands near the flames.

Bob relaxed and took his hand off the Ruger, at the same time, pulling part of the bag over it. "Just tonight," he said and took a quick sip of the coffee. "What about you?"

"I live about half a mile away," Aaron replied.

"Is that right?" Bob sniffed, then asked, "What are you doing in the woods?"

"Oh … I was watching out for some characters that have been ransacking some of the cottages on the lake. I thought I saw some lights a while ago. Just thought I'd check things out."

Bob sensed that the boy was not dangerous in any way. He appeared a bit haggard, but he had a soothing voice and didn't appear nervous. "So you live on the lake?" Bob asked.

"Kinda," said Aaron.

"Then you must know the people."

"Not too well, actually," Aaron confessed.

"You live with your family?"

"Uh … no. Just me."

"Just you?" asked Bob. He took another sip of the coffee. "What do you do? You got a job?"

"Not exactly," said Aaron. "I do a little fishing … a little trapping … I get by."

"You're kinda young to be out on your own, aren't you?"

Aaron looked over at Bob. "I'm eighteen," he said.

"What did you do … run away from home?" Bob guessed. Aaron didn't answer. There was a long silence, and then Bob asked him, "Ever heard of a place called The Lake House?"

Aaron found a dry stick on the ground and fed it to the fire. "Of course. I mean, there are plenty of lake houses on Lake Minocqua."

"I'm looking for one particular place," Bob revealed.

"Well, I don't really know anybody here," said Aaron.

"How long have you lived here?" asked Bob.

"Oh … just a month or so."

"I see." Bob drank more of his coffee. Then he said, "I had a visit from those so-called characters you were telling about."

"You did?"

"They came around my car a while ago. I was trying to sleep in the back seat."

"Did they see you?"

"Nope. A girl called them away. She needed them to help her … whatever she'd been up to. It didn't sound good."

"I've been hoping to catch them," said Aaron. "They've been vandalizing and causing all kinds of damage to the area. They're SDS members."

"What's that? SDS?" asked Bob.

Aaron explained about the demonstrators on college campuses who were protesting against the Vietnamese war. "One of 'em's wanted for some crime," he explained. "They're radicals."

"I see," said Bob.

"Well, I'd better get back to my shack." Aaron stood up and brushed himself off.

"I think I know why you're hiding out here at the lake," said Bob.

Aaron looked startled. "What?"

"Are you heading up to Canada, by any chance?"

"Uh … I was." Aaron hung his head.

"Are you a draft dodger?"

"Uh … you could say that, I guess."

"Then Canada's your best bet. You don't want to go to Vietnam."

Aaron lingered, his hands in his coat pockets. "Hey, were you over there? In the war?"

"Yup." Bob stared into the fire. "I almost didn't make it back."

Aaron crouched down next to Bob and said, "I'd like to shake your hand."

"Why?"

"Because I admire you for your bravery. I want to thank you for your service."

Startled, Bob set down his coffee cup and let the boy shake his hand.

15

The Cabin in the Woods

Annette was wet and miserable. They had been trudging through the dark woods for half an hour. Ruby was whimpering and Penny was up ahead, having an argument with Fern, convinced that the older girl was leading them in the wrong direction. "There's no road," cried Penny. "You said there was a road."

"I *thought* there was a road," argued Fern.

"Well, we'd better find some shelter soon. Boy, are we gonna be in trouble when we get back to the lake house."

"I really am sorry," said Fern. "Would you rather have capsized in the middle of the lake?"

"Do you have any idea which direction we're going?" asked Penny.

"No," said Fern. "We're lost. Are you satisfied?"

Annette called out, "Cut it out, you two."

Ruby clung to Annette's arm and now shook it. "Annette, I think I see a light through those trees."

"Where?"

Ruby pointed off to the left, where Annette caught a glimpse of an orange light flickering through the tree branches. She wasn't sure what kind of light it was, but she stopped and called to Fern and Penny. "A light!"

The girls turned around and they all stood, bunched up, craning their necks to see through the woods. "I see it," said Fern. "It looks like we've found a cabin. Come on."

Everyone followed Fern as she plowed her way through brush, moving slowly because there was very little light to see anything. The clouds were breaking up and the moon was out, but it wasn't very full. The beam from her little penlight was fading fast.

"Okay, Ruby?" Annette asked.

"I'm so cold," said the girl.

"We're almost there."

Five minutes later, they reached a dwelling, obviously a recreational cabin that was a ways from the lake. Fern didn't recognize the area, but she knew there must be a road or at least a trail leading somewhere away from the cabin. The light they had seen was no longer on.

"Maybe they're sleeping," said Ruby.

"Come on." Penny urged them around the side of the cabin to what looked like the front entrance. It was a rustic old cabin with a loft, and Fern walked up to the front door and tried the knob. To their surprise, the cabin was unlocked.

"Oh, thank goodness," said Annette. Fern was a little hesitant to walk in, but after a moment she opened the door wide and all four of them stepped inside the dark room.

"Anybody home?" called Fern in a loud voice. Her weak flashlight beam indicated a furnished living room with cushioned chairs, a bear rug in front of a fireplace that had burned down to orange coals. There was a small table with rickety wooden chairs and a stack of firewood in the corner. A doorway opened into a tiny kitchen next to a ladder that went up to the loft, which was the sleeping area.

"Hello ..." Fern called out again.

There was no answer. "I'll see if I can get some light so we can see," said Penny, groping around in the dark.

"There's probably no electricity," said Fern. "This place is really remote. I'm sure it's a vacation cabin." Her dim flashlight beam showed some fishing rods and gear leaning in one corner of the room. "And I don't think anyone's here."

"Then what was that light we saw?" Annette was shivering. She and Ruby walked over to the fireplace, seeking warmth.

"That is kind of weird," admitted Fern.

"Maybe there are other cabins around," suggested Penny.

"Let's build up the fire first," said Ruby, kneeling down to remove the screen. She began putting small pieces of tinder onto the coals.

"Well, someone must have been here," said Annette. "At least they had a fire going."

"You're right about that," said Fern.

Penny wandered over to the doorway that led into the kitchen and disappeared. They could hear her bumping into things in the dark.

"Well, at least we've got some shelter till we can decide what to do," added Fern.

"I wonder if there's a telephone," said Ruby, looking up from her fire-building task.

"Not likely," replied Fern.

"Hey, there's a Coleman lantern in here," Penny called from the kitchen. "Anyone know how to work it?"

"I do." Fern quickly sauntered off while Annette bent down and helped Ruby with getting the fire started. The wood caught quickly, and soon flames were leaping up and warming them.

"How are we gonna get back to the lake house?" Ruby asked Annette. "Won't they be worried about us?"

"I'm sure they are," said Annette, "but now we'll probably have to wait till morning, when we can figure out where we are and how to get back there … or to the lake, where we left the canoe."

Fern and Penny started laughing and soon they emerged. Penny held the Coleman lantern up and illuminated the room as Fern followed after her. Both girls collapsed into two shabby cushioned chairs, and Penny set the lantern on an end table. It hummed as it burned, and the fire was starting to warm things up.

"This place is a mess," commented Ruby, who sat on top of the bear rug next to the fireplace. They all looked around the room and saw that it was indeed a shambles. When they had first come in, they hadn't seen all the clutter of things scattered around. There were heaps of things, as if someone had just moved in and hadn't unpacked yet.

"Look at this stuff," said Annette as she walked around and examined some of the piles. "Why, there's good stuff here … it looks like silverware … camping gear … paintings … and food!"

Penny got up and started rummaging through some of the stuff. "Maybe there's something to eat in here," she said.

"I found some blankets and pillows," said Annette, pulling them out of a large box.

"Hey, there's jewelry in here," said Penny, pulling out a wooden carved box. The lid was already open, and the box was jammed with gold watches, necklaces, earrings and expensive-looking bracelets made of gold and silver.

"Good grief," said Fern, coming over to have a look. "Who leaves stuff like this out? And their door unlocked?"

"That's a good question," said Annette, gazing around and realizing that most of the stuff in this cabin seemed out of place for a fisherman or a hunter, or even a family coming for a cozy weekend in the woods. "It's starting to give me the creeps."

Fern and Penny looked at her. "What do you mean,

Annette?"

Annette looked into a few more of the boxes and bags and nodded her head. Then she said, "This looks to me like a lot of loot."

"Loot?" asked Ruby.

"Yes," said Annette, "as in … stolen goods."

Fern and Penny gasped. "Oh my gosh," Penny said, "this might be a hide-out."

"I'm scared," said Ruby.

"You mean, somebody's been robbing the area and using this cabin?"

"It certainly looks that way," said Annette, "and if I'm right, I have a hunch they'll be back. Maybe sooner than later."

"We can't stay here?" Ruby looked ready to cry. "I was just getting warm."

"We don't know anything for sure," said Fern.

"But they must have been here recently," said Penny, "because the coals were still hot in the fireplace."

"And the light you saw." Annette looked at Ruby. "They might have just left."

"To go rob somebody!" cried Penny. "Oh, no … what are we gonna do?"

"Don't panic," said Fern. "I think you're jumping to conclusions. Most likely, somebody just moved in."

"Yeah, right," Penny grunted, "and they had to bring all their silver and jewelry with them to the woods."

"Stop it, you two," chided Annette, trying to think. "Our main concern right now is getting help so we can get back to the lake house. Penny, you and Fern should go outside with the lantern and see if there are any neighboring cabins around."

"That sounds like a good idea," Penny agreed.

"But what if you and Ruby are here and the thieves come back?" Fern worried.

"We'll just have to take that chance," said Annette. She brought one of the blankets to wrap around Ruby, who stared into the fire, just glad to be warm again.

"Okay," said Fern. "Penny and I are going out. We'll be right back if we can't find any cabins."

"I wish we'd stayed at the lake house this afternoon," Penny grumbled as she followed Annette's cousin out the door.

"This is some spring break, isn't it, Annette?" Ruby tried to smile, but there were tears in her eyes. "If the robbers come back, are they going to kill us?" She gulped.

"Oh, Ruby, don't think that way. Of course not." Annette sighed, then added, "We're gonna be all right. Don't you worry."

Her words might have comforted Ruby, but not Annette. She knew the situation was a dangerous one, and they were helpless if the looters returned and found them there. But she had been in dangerous situations before. She walked over to the boxes and searched until she found something she could use … just in case.

16

Distressed

"It's too late to call now, they're closed," said Aunt Marie as she hung up the telephone at the reception desk, "but I thought I'd call the Chamber of Commerce, in case somebody came in, looking for information on lodges in this area."

"Well, that's an idea," said Mrs. Vetter. "What did the sheriff's office say?"

"A deputy is coming over." She called to Uncle Joe, who was getting a heavier jacket to wear. "Help is on its way," she told him.

"I need to make a long-distance call," said Mrs. Vetter.

"Of course, Helen … go ahead." Aunt Marie stepped away from the phone.

Terry and Uncle Joe were getting bundled up to go search again for the missing girls and their canoe. Mrs. Vetter had to search her purse to find the little address book she carried. She looked up the number she needed and dialed direct.

After two rings, a familiar voice answered, "This is Will."

Mrs. Vetter was relieved to have finally reached him. "Will, it's Helen."

"Helen! My gosh!" Will grew excited. "I tried to reach you again today after I got home from work. I tried yesterday …"

"I know about that," she said, interrupting him. "Will, Tim said that Bob came by yesterday morning."

"Yes, that's why I tried to call you," said Will.

"I'm in Minocqua," she explained. "Saturday I drove the girls and Terry up to my sister's lake house. Apparently Bob showed up in Ravensville sometime yesterday morning. We didn't find out about him until today."

Uncle Will explained how Bob Foley had surprised him Saturday morning and had spent the night with him in Madison. He added that Bob had driven without stopping from Colorado Springs and had needed a good night's sleep. "I told Bob I'd call you, to let you know he was coming."

"Will, I can't believe it. Bob Foley's alive!"

"Yes," said Will. Then, after a pause, he asked, "He's not there?"

"Why, no," said Mrs. Vetter. "We think he might be in the vicinity, though. Bob found out from Tim that we were in Minocqua, but Tim didn't have any detailed information for him. We don't know where he is."

"Does Ruby know?"

Mrs. Vetter almost sobbed, but caught herself. "No ..."

"Helen, I'm sorry ... it had to have been a shock."

"No, Will ... it's not that." She sniffed. "It's something else ... the girls are missing."

"What!"

"Terry and I drove back up this afternoon," she explained, "and apparently my niece took the three girls out in the canoe a few hours ago. A storm came up suddenly and they didn't return. Now it's dark ... and ... oh dear!"

"Helen, I'm sorry," said Will. "Is there anything I can do?"

"Marie called the sheriff," she explained. "A deputy is on his way. Joe and Terry went out to search again. We're all very concerned."

"Of course," said Will. "I am too. Those kids mean every-thing to me."

"I know. Me too." Mrs. Vetter stifled another sob. "Well, I won't keep you."

"Please call me, Helen, when you know anything," Will pleaded. She told him she would, then ended the conversation.

"I have a casserole warming in the kitchen," said Aunt Marie. "Maybe we should go ahead and eat something. You must be tired and hungry after that long drive."

"Thank you, Marie, but I don't think I could eat a bite."

Her sister put her arm around her, then led Annette's mother into the big room with the fireplace, where they sat down and waited for the deputy sheriff to arrive.

After the boy, Aaron, had left his campfire, Bob sat and collected his thoughts. At one time he would have reacted differently to a young man who had burned his draft card and was neglecting his obligation to serve his country. But this young man seemed different. He hadn't appeared cocky or impolite. He had been straightforward in saying exactly how he felt, without mincing words or trying to act innocent. He had even shown respect.

Bob heated another cup of water and decided to have more instant coffee. Sleep would not be coming for some time, and he had to think of how he was going to find the kids tomorrow, even if he had to drive to every lodge, every resort on every lake. It was only right that they know he was alive. But he questioned his role in their lives now. He wanted Ruby to be happy.

Fern and Penny had ventured out from the cabin in the woods, determined to find another dwelling or even a road. They now had the lantern to see with, and after they had walked about a quarter of a mile, they realized they had made no progress in that direction.

"Let's swing over this way," Fern suggested, leading Penny off to the right. "I think the lake's in this direction."

"Well, okay," said Penny, looking around at the trees and expecting to see some wild animal's eyes lit up and staring back at her.

"I'm glad it quit raining at least," said Fern.

"I see a few stars up above," said Penny, shielding her eyes from the glare of the lantern.

"There's still some clouds," said Fern, "or I'd be able to tell which direction we're headed if we could see more stars and the constellations."

"The stars are so much brighter up here in the North," said Penny. "You're lucky to live in such a beautiful area."

"We get a lot of snow in the winter," said Fern.

Penny laughed. "Well, we get quite a bit too. It is Wisconsin, after all."

Fern suddenly stopped and Penny almost ran into her. "Somebody's up ahead," Fern said in a whisper.

"Where?" whispered Penny.

"I saw a flashlight."

"Maybe we should shout or something," said Penny.

"No," warned Fern. "We don't know who it is."

"Oh, you mean … it could be … the robbers?"

"Aaron said there were three older kids from Chicago ransacking some of the cabins. What if it's them?"

Instinctively, the two girls crouched behind a big ever-green. Fern set the lantern down on the ground and turned the knob until it was off. Then they waited to see what would happen next.

Several minutes passed and Penny hugged herself from the cold. "Where did they go?" she whispered.

Fern sighed. "I'm not sure. *Wait* … there's that flashlight again …"

"Where?" Penny then saw in the distance somebody walking in the woods. They tried to stay very still.

Suddenly, a movement in the brush behind them startled Penny and she jumped. Fern reacted and accidentally caused the lantern to fall, which made a clanking sound on a rock. The person with the flashlight stopped ahead and slowly turned the beam of light in their direction.

"What's that smell?" Penny whispered as she leaned closer to the older girl. "It's kind of rank …"

"Oh, no," Fern whispered back. "I smell it too."

A movement behind them rustled the bushes again and this time they heard a deep growl. "Penny … don't move." Fern's voice was trembling. She grabbed hold of the lantern on the ground and then slowly held it close to her body.

"What … is … it?" Penny feared the worst.

A louder growl sounded, and suddenly the person holding the flashlight started to walk away … rapidly. The girls huddled together as a huge hairy animal sprang past them and lunged toward the person now running with the flashlight.

"It's a bear!" Penny struggled to keep her voice low, but she was in panic mode.

"Come on, let's get out of here." Fern picked up the lantern and took off in the direction they had come. Penny was at her heels, stumbling in the dark.

They heard a male voice let out a scream, but they didn't wait around to see the outcome. The girls had run about fifty yards when they heard a female voice shouting, and then there came a gunshot—not once, but three times—in the vicinity of the bear chasing the person with the flashlight. The next thing they heard was the girl's scream.

Fern and Penny beat it back to the fishing cabin as fast as they could in the dark, without the aid of the lantern. Fern was afraid to stop and light it, and Penny preferred to stumble in the dark than get eaten by a bear. Finally, when they saw the flicker of firelight in a window of the cabin, they knew they were close.

Annette was standing with the door open as they came running, her eyes wide with fear. "Are you guys all right? I heard shots."

"There's a bear!" cried Penny, falling inside, Fern right behind her. "Close the door!"

Ruby, still sitting by the fire, quickly stood up.

"It was a black bear," Fern panted, equally frightened. At the second mention, Ruby shrieked and Annette quickly shut the door.

"There were some other people out there," Penny explained, still trying to catch her breath. "The bear ran right past us ... maybe somebody shot it."

"Or maybe they got mauled," Fern added.

"I want to go home," Ruby sobbed. "What if the bear comes *here?*"

Annette turned to comfort the girl. "Ruby, you're safe in here. The bear is not coming inside this cabin." She faced Fern and Penny. "I think we'd better plan on spending the night here."

"Good idea," said Penny, collapsing into one of the cushioned chairs.

Fern got the Coleman lantern lit once again and looked around. "It's going to be a long night," she said. "Oh, how I wish Aaron was here with us." She began to cry.

Suddenly, there was a knock on the front door of the cabin.

The four girls gasped at once. Fern was the first one to jump up. "Maybe it's him," she said hopefully, hurrying to the door. "Maybe Aaron's here. He'll help us."

Annette and Penny exchanged glances. Annette was thinking, what if it *wasn't* Aaron? What if it was one of the thieves? She reached under the blanket next to the fireplace, where she had hidden the hatchet she had found. Just in case …

When Fern opened the door to the cabin, she cried out, "Aaron?" Then she gasped. "Who are *you*?" She backed away as a tall silhouette stood at the entry and started to move inside.

Annette gripped the hatchet and stood up, ready to use it if she had to.

17

The Man at the Door

The sheriff's deputy finally arrived at the lake house an hour after Aunt Marie had called for help. Uncle Joe and Terry were out in the woods, searching. The deputy, who introduced himself as Alex Brodsky, apologized for the delay but gave no excuse. He asked questions and took notes.

"Teen-agers are known for this kind of thing," he told the women as if it were an everyday affair when girls went out on the lake in a canoe and didn't come home.

"But there was that storm," insisted Aunt Marie. "We're very worried."

"When your daughter goes out on the lake, how long is she usually gone?" asked the deputy.

"Oh, I'd say ... well, sometimes a couple of hours, some-times three. But she knows the lake, officer. It isn't like her to not come home before twilight. It's going on nine o'clock."

"And what time did they venture out?" He sounded bored, which irritated the women.

"I don't know ... it was three-thirty or four after we got home from town," said Aunt Marie. "We need to get some people out there looking. They could have capsized in that storm. There's no telling what could have happened to the girls."

Mrs. Vetter was trying to hold back tears. At that moment, Uncle Joe and Terry came in from outside and turned their flashlights off.

"Hello, deputy," called out Uncle Joe.

Before Alex could reply, his walky-talky radio crackled and a voice came through, paging him. With a sigh, he reached for it and pushed the button. "Brodsky here."

The staticky voice was undecipherable.

"Excuse me a minute," said the deputy and walked outside where he thought the reception might be better. No one could make out what the dispatcher was saying, but as he went out the door, they heard him say, "Roger."

"No luck?" Aunt Marie blinked her eyes in despair as Uncle Joe shook his head.

"Are the police gonna help us?" Terry asked hopefully.

Her arms crossed in dismay, Mrs. Vetter shook her head.

"Is there some coffee?" Uncle Joe started for the kitchen.

"No, but I'll make some." Aunt Marie followed after him.

"Mom …" Terry put his arm around Mrs. Vetter. "Don't worry. We'll find them."

Suddenly, the deputy came back inside. "Somebody reported some gunfire on the other side of the lake," he reported. "I'm going to check it out."

Uncle Joe had heard him and rushed in from the kitchen. "Wait. I'll come along."

"I want to come too," said Terry.

"You should stay here with your mother," said Uncle Joe.

"Please, Uncle Joe …"

Mrs. Vetter nodded. "Joe, let him go along."

Terry and Uncle Joe followed Deputy Brodsky out the front door, and Mrs. Vetter went into the kitchen to tell Aunt Marie the latest.

"Gunfire?"

"It might not have anything to do with the girls," said

Mrs. Vetter.

"Oh, Helen … this is all my fault. I give Fern way too much freedom. Joe always says…"

"Nonsense." Mrs. Vetter reached out for her sister. "Fern's almost a grown woman. She has good common sense."

"Gunfire …" Aunt Marie broke down at that point, and the two sisters sat at the kitchen table to comfort each other and wait for some news.

A aron had been walking back to his shack on the far side of the swamp when he heard shots being fired. There were some isolated cabins off the beaten track and it sounded as if the gunfire had come from that direction. He took a short-cut through the woods, and as he got closer, he heard a girl sobbing up ahead. He picked up his pace.

His flashlight picked up two familiar figures standing outside an empty cabin. The blonde girl was the one he'd seen before with the two agitators that had tried to bully him into joining them. The red-haired, shorter guy was kneeling over a bulky mass of black fur that was lying in a pool of blood. Aaron stopped in front of an injured black bear.

"What happened here?" asked Aaron, his flashlight beam taking it all in. "Is it dead?"

"Not yet," said the redhead with a frown.

"Who shot it?" asked Aaron.

The girl scowled at him. "I did. It was coming after Darrell," she snarled. "It would have killed him. I had to do something."

Aaron saw that a .22 rifle lay on the ground at her feet. He didn't know that much about guns, but his best buddy in high school had gone hunting a lot with his dad, and Aaron had been told that a .22 wouldn't kill a bear … not easily, anyway.

He stared at the girl, then said, "You've only stunned it. I suggest we move away … before it regains its strength and comes after us."

The red-headed guy immediately jumped back, but Brenda put her hands on her hips. "Look at the blood," she said sarcastically. "*I* did that! Me! I shot the bear." She grinned.

"There's nothing more dangerous than a wounded bear," Aaron warned her.

"Brenda, maybe he's right." The redhead tried to pull the girl away from the mass of suffering black flesh on the ground.

"Nick, you jerk ... go find Darrell!" She looked around. "What happened to him, anyway?"

"If he was smart, he ran away," commented Aaron.

"Nobody asked *you*, draft dodger," Brenda snapped. "You'd best be on your way, or I might have to give you a reason ..." She kicked at the rifle on the ground.

Loud grunts came from the wounded bear just then. Aaron, without saying another word, turned around and almost ran smack into Darrell, the tall, dark-headed leader of the trio.

"So ... it's you," the leader said to Aaron, getting right in his face. "I think we have some unfinished business."

"I'm leaving," said Aaron and tried to sidestep Darrell.

"No, you're not." Nick came up behind and Aaron was trapped on all sides—Darrell in front, Nick behind, Brenda on one side, and the injured, writhing, bleeding bear on the other.

Fern stood frozen at the front door of the cabin while Penny joined Annette and Ruby, who huddled together in fear next to the fireplace. Even with the lantern light, which glowed from a corner of the room, they could not see who the figure was standing outside the door.

"Sorry to barge in on you," a man's voice said. "I'm camping on the lake just a short ways from here, and I happened to hear shots fired."

"Uh ..." Fern stepped back and glanced over at the three

girls. When Annette nodded with consent, Fern sighed and said, "We … we heard them too."

Then Penny stepped forward and burst out, "There was a bear!" She confronted the man at the door, her green eyes wide with fear. "Out in the woods!"

"A bear?" the man asked. "Where?"

Penny lost her fear of the visitor in her excitement over their escapade. "We ran … but somebody else fired the gun. We don't know who."

Annette left Ruby's side and slowly approached the door. She studied the figure in the dark entrance. He was a tall man wearing baggy pants and an Air Force jacket, the hood pulled up over his head. She stood next to the other two girls, the hatchet hidden behind her back.

"Can you tell us if there's a road nearby?" Annette asked.

"Yeah, it's not too far from here," the man said, puzzled by her question. His eyes squinted with suspicion. "Where are your parents?"

"Uh …" Fern looked at the others, afraid to answer for fear the man, being a stranger, might try something.

"Never mind," the man said. "I just thought somebody might be in trouble. I'm sorry to bother you." He turned to go out the door.

"Wait, mister!" Ruby shouted. The blonde girl stepped forward from the fireplace. "We need your help." She boldly walked over to join the rest of them. "Can you drive us back to the lake house?"

"Shhh, *Ruby!*" Fern scolded the girl.

"Lake house?" The man at the door stepped inside and the full lantern light illuminated his face. Then his eyes grew wide as they fell on the 13-year-old with the blonde hair.

"It's okay," said Annette, drawing her sister protectively beside her with her free hand. "She's right, sir. We do need help."

"We have to get back to the lake house," Ruby explained, and then suddenly her blue eyes widened in disbelief as they met the man's blue eyes. She gasped, then a cry escaped from her. "Oh!"

"Ruby?" the man muttered, his voice shaking. He slowly pushed the hood back off his head, revealing brown hair and a scar over his right eye.

"D-d-Daddy?" Ruby moved away from Annette and hesitantly approached the man at the door. Then, with a grin on her face, she spun around and looked up at Annette. "Annette, it's my father!"

"What?" cried Penny.

"Ruby!" The man at the door bent forward and reached his arms out toward the girl, and to the surprise of the others, Ruby fell into them and began bawling.

"It's my *dad* ... it's really my dad!"

"Ruby ... my little girl ..." Bob was sobbing as well.

The three older girls stood in place, stunned. Finally, Fern motioned them to come inside so she could close the door, which was letting in too much cold air.

Bob Foley stood up with Ruby still clinging to him, then moved further into the room, tears streaking down his face.

Annette noticed right away the man was limping. She lay the hatchet down on one of the crates, then stood aside with her cousin and her best friend as Bob took a seat in one of the cushioned chairs and the blonde girl climbed onto his lap.

"You're Ruby's father?" Annette asked in amazement.

Bob, wiping tears from his eyes, merely nodded his head.

Ruby's sobs finally subsided and she asked, "Daddy, I can't believe you're really here. How did you find me?"

The older girls gathered around to hear his story.

"Uncle Will said you and Terry were living in Ravensville," Bob explained. "I drove up from Madison on Sunday morning, but the neighbor boy said you'd gone to

Minocqua for spring break. I've been looking for the lake house … and now fate has led me here."

"Tim must have told him," Penny whispered to Annette, who nodded.

"Daddy, this isn't the lake house," Ruby explained, wiping her nose. She laughed. "The lake house we're staying at is on the other side of the lake."

Baffled, Bob looked to Annette for help. She explained, "We got caught in a storm on the lake, and we ended up having to come to shore. We walked awhile before we found this cabin. It was dark and we had no idea where the road is."

"Actually, you're not too far from the road," said Bob. "My car is parked at the lake just a ways from here."

"But Daddy!" cried Ruby. "How did you know we were here in this cabin?"

"I didn't know, Ruby. I came only because I heard the shots. I thought somebody was in trouble."

"What a coincidence," Penny said in awe. Then she added, "Gee, we should have told Tim how to reach us."

"Tim is Penny's brother," explained Annette to Bob. "He was taking care of the cows for us."

Bob said, "He didn't have a phone number or a name. Do you know how many lake houses there are in Minocqua?"

"Plenty," said Fern, rolling her dark eyes. "Ours is called Parkers' Lake House."

"That's because Aunt Marie and Uncle Joe's last name is Parker," Ruby told her dad.

All of them were still rather stunned that Ruby's missing father was there with them. Tears of happiness streamed down Bob's cheeks as he hugged Ruby, who didn't want to let go of him either. Annette had a thousand questions she wanted to ask, but now was not the right time.

Outside the cabin window, she saw the flash of red and blue lights. Peeking out the glass, she saw a police car driving up the road that Bob Foley had told them existed nearby.

"Looks like help has arrived," said Penny excitedly. Fern picked up the Coleman lantern, and they all stood up and started heading for the door.

"Wait ... it's driving away!" cried Annette.

Sure enough, the red and blue lights were speeding off up the road.

"We can walk back to my campsite," Bob told the girls. "I'll drive you back to where you're staying."

Ruby clung to her father, not wanting to let go as they left the cabin. With a glance over her shoulder, Annette noted that the fire had died down in the fireplace, and she breathed a sigh of relief that the robbers had not returned. Maybe the police were responding to a call about them at one of the cabins up the road.

Terry and Uncle Joe rode in the back seat of Alex Brodsky's patrol car. They were now in the vicinity of where the gunshots had been reported. They learned from the deputy that some tourists staying in one of the cottages on the lake had called in, using their citizens' band radio, but nobody knew exactly where the location was.

"Probably just a false alarm," Alex commented in his lackadaisical voice. "Most likely just somebody target shooting."

"At night?" Uncle Joe was dubious.

"But we'll check it out," said the officer. "There are some more cabins up ahead."

"Not too many people around," mentioned Terry, looking out the windows. All he could see were trees and a glimpse of the lake every now and then. The partial moon was out and causing a reflection on the lake, although the road was taking them farther away from the water.

"It's still off season," said Uncle Joe. "A few people here for Easter weekend, but we don't really start getting tourists till May first."

"I hope we find the girls," said Terry. "I don't want to think about them spending the night in the woods. Maybe we should check some of these cabins."

"They could be anywhere," said Uncle Joe. "We have no idea what happened, whether they beached the canoe and started walking ..." He sighed in frustration.

"How long would it take to walk around the lake?" asked Terry. The deputy shrugged.

"Fern's got common sense," said Uncle Joe. "I just hope ..." He couldn't say it.

Suddenly, without warning, a human figure darted out in front of the patrol car as it was speeding down the road in the dark woods. Terry screamed, "Look out!"

The deputy swerved quickly to the right, narrowly missing the person in the road, but then something huge crashed into the right side of the squad car, sending it rocking toward the left side of the road.

With squealing brakes, the police vehicle struck a large evergreen trunk and the occupants inside were thrown forward.

18

Attacked!

Terry had blacked out for a few moments, but when he
came to, he saw that the police car was tilted and smashed
in on the front passenger side. Luckily, no one had been in that
seat. Uncle Joe was in the back seat beside him, leaning against
his door, not moving. Deputy Brodsky was moaning behind
the wheel in front, possibly hurt.

"Uncle Joe!" Terry soon realized the man beside him was
unconscious. He noticed a commotion outside of the car. Terry
was having trouble seeing what was going on in the dark, even
though the headlights of the patrol car were still on. Both
beams tilted up at an angle against a huge evergreen that was
bracing the cracked windshield.

Then he heard a voice outside, screaming, and a loud
snarling animal. A black bear was outside the car, tumbling
around on the ground, slamming against the metal of the
trunk. Glancing out the back window, Terry was sure he saw
somebody running around in the trees nearby, and he heard
cries for help that sounded muffled.

"We hit a bear!" Terry shouted at Deputy Brodsky.
"Uncle Joe, wake up!"

The deputy seemed to be coming around. "What ... oh,

my head ... what ... who ..."

"Does your radio work?" Terry leaned over the back of the front seat. "Can you call for help? There's a bear mauling somebody outside your squad car."

Uncle Joe stirred in the back seat and seemed to be coming around. The deputy didn't answer.

A male voice screamed desperately from outside the car, followed by more thumping and vicious growls from the excited animal.

"Bear attack!" Terry grabbed hold of Uncle Joe's shoulders and gently shook him. "Wake up, Uncle Joe. Please!"

"Terry ..." Uncle Joe's eyes fluttered open. He looked around and blinked, then asked, "Are you hurt?"

"No, just shook up."

Uncle Joe was able to move his head and he looked out the window and could see what was happening in the darkness. "Somebody's in big trouble."

"I'm getting out." Terry tried his door handle, but it didn't work. Then he remembered that most cop cars didn't open from the inside of the back seat.

"No, stay in the car," ordered Uncle Joe. He reached over the seat to check on Deputy Brodsky. "Hey ... are you okay, Alex?"

The deputy could only moan. A voice came through the car radio, but it was mostly static. Alex stirred again and was trying to stay conscious. "Backup ... we need backup," he mumbled.

"That's an understatement," said Uncle Joe. "Terry, can you reach into the front seat? Don't open that door till I say." His voice was firm.

The squad car was tilted at an angle that made it difficult for Terry to get his balance, but he struggled until he was able to slip his body into the bashed-in passenger side of the front seat. He managed to grab the deputy's microphone and pushed the "talk" button.

"Breaker, breaker ..." Terry wasn't sure what words to use, but those were the only ones that came to his mind at the moment. "We need help. The deputy's squad car hit a tree. He's injured. We need help *now*."

The only thing that came through was more static. Terry tried again, but it was no use. The deputy had passed out. Uncle Joe was busy watching out the back window.

"The bear just took off," said Uncle Joe.

"I'm getting out," said Terry.

"Careful!" ordered Uncle Joe. "The animal might come back."

Terry then realized he couldn't open the passenger door because it was smashed in and the handle didn't work. The only escape was out the driver's door, and Deputy Brodsky was slumped over the wheel, unconscious. "I can't get out," cried Terry.

"Don't panic, son." Uncle Joe was breathing hard.

"Should I move him?" Terry asked, edging closer to Alex.

"I wouldn't," said Uncle Joe. "Hold on. I'll think of something ..."

Then somebody was yelling outside the car. Terry and Uncle Joe looked out the side window and saw another figure approaching the deputy's car. A young man with scraggly long hair and glasses peered inside the window, then tried to open the door handle, but it was stuck. Next, he tried the back door and was able to yank it open after several tries.

Terry climbed back over the seat and hopped out through the back door, and Uncle Joe wiggled his body over and stumbled out after him.

"Anybody hurt?" asked the young man who had rescued them, his eyes wide.

"The deputy," said Terry, pointing. He wiped some blood off his chin, where he'd gotten cut from some glass.

Uncle Joe stood, staring down at something beside the car. Terry and the young man saw that it was a chubby older boy. His blue down jacket was covered with blood, and he lay face down, not moving.

"That bear might come back," warned Uncle Joe.

"There's a cabin down the road that you passed," said the long-haired guy with glasses, "and there's a house in the other direction that was just robbed."

"Robbed?" Terry looked at him, uncertain.

"Yeah, I was trying to stop the thieves. They've been raiding vacation homes. This dude on the ground is one of 'em."

"He needs to get to a hospital," declared Terry, who knelt beside the boy.

"Where are the others?" asked Uncle Joe.

"A girl named Brenda and her boyfriend Darrell … they took off, heading toward that other cabin. They have a rifle."

"And who are you?" asked Uncle Joe.

"My name's Aaron."

"Well, Aaron, we need to get help and fast."

"Yes, sir."

"Are we gonna leave them?" Terry asked, indicating the deputy in the car and the injured boy on the ground.

"Maybe one of us should stay here," said Aaron.

"Do any of those cabins have telephones?" asked Uncle Joe.

Aaron shrugged. "I doubt it. They're mostly fishermen's shacks. No electricity."

"I'll stay here with them," Terry volunteered.

Uncle Joe sighed, but then gave in. "Get inside the car and stay there, in case that bear comes back," he told Terry. Then he added, "Keep trying the radio."

Terry nodded, then opened the back door and climbed back inside. He watched as Aaron and Uncle Joe hurried back down the road. He prayed they would succeed in getting help. He crawled back into the front seat to check on Alex, who was groaning and coming around once again. Grabbing the microphone, Terry decided to keep trying to radio in for assistance.

Annette followed the others out of the dark cabin into the wet woods. Bob Foley held Ruby's hand and led the way toward the road that earlier they hadn't realized was there. Penny and Fern walked together, just ahead of her, and nobody talked. All they could think about was getting to safety, warmth and light. Annette couldn't concentrate on Bob Foley's return. She felt as though she was in a dream, and she wished she could wake up.

They hadn't gone very far when running footsteps met Annette's ears. She halted as the others in front of her kept on going, apparently unaware of the sound. Nobody turned to see if she was keeping up. She quickly hid herself behind a tree and waited to see who was running through the forest.

Soon she made out two figures breathing hard and carrying large cloth sacks. They headed toward the cabin where the girls had taken refuge. Annette carefully followed them, darting from tree to tree and keeping a safe distance, so that they wouldn't see her.

The two halted in front of the cabin door and set their sacks on the ground. Annette saw that one was a young woman and the other a taller, dark-haired guy. The girl propped what looked like a rifle up against the wall of the cabin, then turned to the young man and he embraced her. She was close enough now to hear what they said.

"I'm so scared," the girl said, her voice shaking.

"It's time for us to split," said the dark-haired guy.

"But what about Nick?" She suddenly burst into tears and buried her head in the young man's shoulder.

"Stop it!" he ordered, pushing her away from him. "Get over it, Brenda. Nick's dead! There's nothing we can do for him. We've gotta get outta here."

"What about our stuff?" Brenda angrily wiped the tears from her eyes and turned to open the cabin door. "We can't leave without the goods. We need Nick's truck."

"The cops have probably found Nick by now," he told her. "I'll go get the truck."

"They're not going to suspect anything, are they?" Brenda asked breathlessly. "Darrell, we've got time to hide the stash at least, then we can come back with the truck."

"I dunno, Brenda. I have a bad feeling. I say we grab the valuables now and go."

She got the cabin door open and the two of them hurried inside. Darrell hesitated to look around first, then closed the door after he went in.

Annette crept closer, being careful not to stumble in the dark as she reached the porch of the cabin. She wondered what they had meant—what had happened to their friend, Nick? They were obviously the three troublemakers Aaron had talked about.

She had no idea how she was going to stop them, but maybe if she overheard their plans, she could relate that information to the police. She crouched under the front window and listened, but their voices weren't loud enough for her to pick up anything.

"Annette!" Penny's voice called from the distance. The sound echoed in the night.

Terrified that Brenda and Darrell inside the cabin might hear her, Annette changed her mind about spying on the thieves. On an impulse, she grabbed the rifle that Brenda had set against the wall next to the door, and ran toward the road. She could see Penny standing in the dark with Fern behind her. Before they could shout anything else, Annette ran toward them.

"Where were you?" demanded Penny, her hands on her hips.

"Where's Ruby and her father?" Annette panted.

"He took her to his campsite," said Fern, indicating the direction they had gone. Annette glimpsed some of the lake from the road. "Where did you get that gun, Annette?" asked Fern.

"Those thieves are in the cabin," she reported, pointing back to the structure. "There are only two of them now. The one named Nick is hurt ... or dead."

Penny gasped.

"What do you mean?" Fern's voice trembled.

"That's what I heard them say."

"Did they see you?" asked Penny.

"I don't think so," said Annette, "but they are going to try to make a getaway tonight. They stole all that stuff in the cabin. It was their hideout, I guess."

"We've got to inform the police," said Penny. "What happened to that squad car with the flashing lights?"

"It drove farther down this road," said Fern. "It's long gone by now. Come on, you two, the best thing we can do now is join Ruby and her father and get back to the lake house."

With a sigh, Annette gripped the rifle in her left hand and joined her cousin and her friend and they walked as fast as they could in the direction of the lake. All three were shivering from the cold night air, not to mention exhausted and hungry. "Bob's car is just a little ways," Fern reassured her.

A thrashing sound came from some nearby bushes along the roadside. Then they all heard a loud grunt and some heavy breathing sounds. Annette's pulse skyrocketed and both Fern and Penny screamed. Annette then saw the big hulk of black bear emerge from the brush, hunched over and staggering a bit, but it was headed right for them.

"That bear is injured," cried Fern.

"Run, Annette!" Penny screamed.

She wasn't even sure the rifle in her hand was loaded.

Annette had never shot a rifle before, but knew she had to take the risk and hope there was a cartridge in the chamber. She backed up against a tree and lifted the firearm to her right shoulder. There was no time to look through the sights and aim. With a sob in her throat, Annette held the rifle and pointed it at the shuffling bear, then squeezed the trigger, clenching her teeth and closing her eyes.

CLICK.

Terror seized Annette and she froze. Penny and Fern were yelling, and the bear was four feet in front of her, but something was wrong with it. She saw a mass of blood on its snout and chest area as ropes of drool streamed from its horrible mouth.

"Annette! Don't move!" somebody shouted. It was a man's voice.

The next thing she heard was an explosion of gunfire. The black bear lurched in front of her. Another deafening shot rang out and the bear dropped to the ground just inches from her feet. The useless rifle dropped from her hands as Annette's head swam and she blacked out.

19

The Note

A circle of heads in the dark surrounded Annette when she opened her eyes and felt the cold air. The rancid odor of an animal pierced her nostrils. As she struggled to sit up, Penny and Fern reached out and pulled Annette up off the ground. She then noticed Ruby standing off a few feet away, her wide blue eyes focused on the large black bear that lay dead at their feet.

Aaron stood next to Fern, his arm around her. "That was some shot," he told the others. "Right between the eyes. Knocked him dead."

"Annette, are you all right?" Penny's face was full of concern.

The scene with the bear and the rifle *not* going off came rushing back to Annette. She blinked her eyes and looked from one face to the other. "But I ... I ... I didn't ... how can the bear be dead?"

"My dad shot him!" Ruby cried out excitedly.

"He did?" Annette looked around, but there was no sign of Bob Foley.

"Come on, let's get her inside the cabin," said Fern, who started to lead Annette away from the dead bear and the blood.

"Yes, it was my dad who shot him," Ruby said, following the rest of them toward the cabin.

"Wait!" cried Annette. "Those two … Brenda and … what's his name?"

"Darrell," said Aaron with a growl. "They ran out of the cabin as soon as they heard the shots."

"That's right," said Penny, "and they took off!"

"Where's Bob Foley?" Annette looked around. "And Aaron … where did you come from?"

"I'll explain it all inside," he promised as they made their way into the building. Fern lit the Coleman lantern again as they all shuffled in out of the cold.

"Aaron and my father were close by and heard the gun-fire," explained Fern. "They ran right over."

"Uncle Joe was here?" Annette looked at Penny, who nodded.

"Then my father and Bob ran after those thieves," Fern added.

"The bear was badly injured when Brenda shot him with that .22," explained Aaron. "I showed up at the scene and they didn't believe me when I told them that bear was more dangerous now that they'd wounded it." He rubbed his hands together and blew into them, then continued, "And when Darrell and Nick ganged up on me over at that other cabin, the bear suddenly rushed on us. It chased Nick and Darrell into the road, and the bear ran right into the side of the oncoming police car."

"My dad and Terry were in that car," said Fern. "The deputy's injured, so Terry stayed with him."

"Terry's back?" asked Annette.

"Yes, apparently your mom and Terry drove back to the lake house this afternoon," explained Fern.

"Is Terry all right?" Annette was frantic with worry over her brother.

"We think so," said Fern.

"I'm heading back there right now," said Aaron.

"Can't we find a way to call for help?" Annette asked.

As if in answer to her remark, they heard sirens. Everyone turned to gaze out the front window, and a moment later they saw a rescue truck and another squad car with flashing lights driving up the road.

"Come on," called Aaron, who was already out the door. The four girls followed him as he led the way up the road toward the crash site. They had to pass the dead bear on the ground and Annette shuddered, remembering the terror she herself had felt only minutes earlier and how close she had come to getting killed by the animal.

When they reached the scene of the accident, the EMTs were extricating Deputy Brodsky from the mangled squad car. Terry had climbed out already and came running over when he saw the girls. He immediately embraced Ruby, then gave Annette a tight hug.

"Thank goodness you're safe," said Annette with tears in her eyes.

"Sergeant, the kid on the road is dead," one of the patrolmen called out. Two officers knelt beside the body of Nick, who had been mangled by the bear behind the squad car.

Fern and Penny backed up, disturbed at the sight, and Aaron led the crowd of friends safely away from the appalling scene as the officers discussed what to do next.

"Terry!" cried Ruby, almost laughing. "Daddy's *alive!* He's here!"

"He is?" Terry had to move out of the way so that the emergency workers could get a stretcher closer to the squad car. He looked at Annette in disbelief. "What is she saying, Annette?"

"Ruby's telling the truth," Annette said with a smile. "Bob Foley showed up at the cabin a while ago. He's alive."

"Oh, I know," said Terry. "Tim told me he stopped by the house Sunday morning. Looks like he found us. So ... where is he? Where's Bob?"

"He shot the bear that was attacking Annette," Ruby exclaimed, "and then he and Uncle Joe ran after those kids that had all their loot in that cabin."

"What loot? What cabin?" Terry was perplexed.

"We'll explain it all later," Penny said, giving Terry a quick hug. "I'm glad you're all right."

Some people from neighboring cabins had shown up with flashlights, and one of the deputies came over to find out what exactly had happened. When they learned that a bear had caused the accident and had mauled the boy who lay dead, the neighbors began talking at once, and looking around nervously in the woods.

Aaron went over to one of the officers who was examining Nick's body and told them about the other two who had been vandalizing the nearby properties and stealing from the cabins. "I can show you where they've hidden the stolen goods," he said.

Penny, Fern and Ruby turned to face Annette and they walked away from the others. "It looks like the police have things under control," said Fern in relief. "I'm so glad Aaron is here."

Terry joined them. "You know Aaron?" he asked Fern.

"He's her boyfriend," Ruby broadcast. At that, Aaron glanced over at them and cracked a smile, then turned his attention back to the police.

"Oh," said Terry. "Well ... it's a good thing he showed up when he did."

"Yes," said Fern with a sigh. "And I think we all need to get back to the lake house. I'm sure Mom and Aunt Helen are worried sick."

"You're absolutely right," said Annette. "Where did

Uncle Joe park the car?" she asked Terry.

"He didn't drive. We rode in the squad car with Deputy Brodsky."

"Oh, that's right …" Annette held her head. "Of course …"

"Annette, are you feeling okay?" Penny looked worried.

"I'm fine."

"We really need to get back to the lake house," Fern told one of the neighbors standing around. "Can anyone give us a lift?"

"I need to find my dad," said Ruby all of a sudden.

"We can stop at his campsite on the way," Penny told the girl. "His car is there. He's bound to show up."

"Come on, I'll take you wherever you need to go," said a middle-aged man in the crowd. "Myrtle," he called to his wife, "we're taking these kids home."

"I'll go bring the station wagon," his wife called to him, and disappeared up the road.

"We're the Snyders," the man said. "I'm Roger and my wife's Myrtle."

"I'm Fern Parker. Pleased to meet you," Fern said and offered her hand for him to shake.

"We met your parents at the chapel on Palm Sunday," said Roger. "We missed the Easter service."

The EMTs finally got the injured deputy into the ambulance. He was conscious now and talking with the paramedics. When Terry asked the police if he or the girls were needed for any further information, they said no, but took their contact information and said they'd be in touch.

About ten minutes later, the Snyders' station wagon pulled up after the kids had started walking down the road. They all piled in with Ruby sitting on Terry's lap and Fern on Aaron's. Annette sat between them while Penny volunteered to sit up front with Roger and Myrtle.

"Can you stop up ahead?" Fern called to the driver.

"Ruby's dad is camped there on the lake."

"Sure," said Roger. But when they got to the designated area, there was no car parked at the campsite. The embers from Bob's campfire were still glowing, and they could see where his car had been parked.

"He's not here," said Penny.

"Where did he go?" asked Ruby.

"Is that his stuff?" Fern pointed out the car window to a pile of camping gear next to the fire.

"Here, I'll get out and see." Ruby moved off her brother's lap so that Terry could get out when the station wagon stopped. He walked over to the pile of gear on the ground and saw that there was a camouflaged backpack. Also, a small thermos had tipped over next to the pack, and he felt around to see what else he could find.

A pen dropped onto the ground, and as Terry lifted the pack, he noticed a sheet of paper lying on the grass. He was going to stuff the paper and pen back into the pack, but then he grabbed everything and carried Bob's things back to the station wagon.

"What is it?" asked Ruby. "Where's Daddy?"

The neighbor man turned on the car's dome light so they could see, and Terry unfolded the paper and read what was on it. Then he handed it to Annette, who read it to everyone out loud:

Dear Kids,

It was important for me to find you. I needed you to know that I was alive and well. I hope to see you again someday. Your happiness means everything to me and I do not want to interfere with your lives now that you have found a family.

When I

"That's it," said Annette. "It ends abruptly."

There was a silence as everyone attempted to absorb the meaning of his words. Then Roger Snyder asked, "What would you like us to do?"

"Maybe he's coming back," cried Ruby. "We need to wait here for him to get back."

"He went with Uncle Joe," said Terry.

"Yes, he probably went to the lake house with my father," Fern said with a smile. "They probably saw that we weren't at the cabin anymore and left on their own."

"I think you should drive us to the lake house," said Terry.

After everyone was settled again, the neighbor man turned off the dome light and continued on down the road that wound around that part of the lake. Annette and the others remained silent. She was tired and overwhelmed with all of the things that had happened since the storm that afternoon. She couldn't wait to get back to the lake house.

Ruby squeezed Annette's hand and smiled up at her. "It's going to be all right," she whispered. "Isn't it?"

Annette simply sighed and stared out into the darkness.

20

Disappointment

M rs. Vetter and Aunt Marie ran out to meet them as soon as the station wagon pulled into the lake house parking area. The yard light was on and the two worried women rushed over with cries of joy. "Oh, thank God, you're safe," said Aunt Marie.

"Is Dad back?" Fern asked her mother as she climbed out, followed by the scraggly-headed Aaron.

Aunt Marie glanced questioningly at the boy standing next to her daughter, then nodded and said, "Yes, he's here. He's inside getting cleaned up."

"What about my dad?" cried Ruby.

Both Mrs. Vetter and Aunt Marie looked surprised.

"We heard Bob found his way here," Terry explained.

Aunt Marie shook her head. "Joe was alone," she said, then turned to Roger and Myrtle, who were looking out the window. Aunt Marie went over to thank them for bringing everyone home.

Mrs. Vetter shook her head sadly. "Bob's not here," she said.

"What did my dad say?" Fern asked. "Bob was with him."

"Yes, we know," said Mrs. Vetter. "Your father said Bob

went back to his campsite to get his gear. But he hasn't shown up."

"But ..." Ruby's face began to collapse. "But then ... oh no ..." She ran toward the front door of the lake house, calling out, "Uncle Joe! Uncle Joe!"

"The police brought Joe home," Aunt Marie told them after the Snyders drove away. "He said there was a bear attack on the other side of the lake, and that a boy was killed."

"That's right," said Fern, and started to tell her mother and her aunt about what happened.

"Let's all go inside," said Aunt Marie. "You girls look like you've been through quite an ordeal. You can tell us what happened, but first, right now you need to go upstairs and wash up ... all of you."

Ruby sauntered back into the lobby, her head hanging down. "He's gone ..."

"Who is?" asked Aunt Marie.

"She saw Bob," Terry said as he came back into the room. "But it appears now that he's left."

Annette, Penny and Fern, who had started up the stairs, turned around and stood, waiting.

"What do you mean he's left?" asked Mrs. Vetter.

"His car was gone when we got back to his campsite," explained Penny.

"And he left this note ..." Terry pulled the folded sheet of paper out of his pocket and handed it to Mrs. Vetter.

Just then, Uncle Joe walked into the room, wiping his forehead with a handkerchief. "Hey, everyone ... looks like those troublemakers are going to be locked up for quite some time." He had everyone gather around in the living room as he told his story.

"After Bob killed that bear, that young couple ran out of the cabin and tried to flee the scene. The two of us ran after them and chased them toward the lake. Unfortunately, Bob can't run very fast … due to his limp … and so it was up to me."

"So what happened?" asked Penny, wide-eyed.

"They finally surrendered," said Uncle Joe. "Bob pulled his gun and they put up their hands. By the time we got back to the road, you all had gone. We marched those two back into the cabin, and Bob guarded them while I flagged down one of the police cars coming up the road. They took Brenda and Darrell into custody."

"Where's my dad now?" Ruby asked Uncle Joe.

"I don't know, Ruby," he said. "I rode in the police car, and Bob said he was going back to his camp to get his car."

"But it was gone when we stopped there," explained Fern. "Where do you think he went?"

"I don't know, honey."

There was a depressing silence, and then Ruby charged upstairs, sobbing. Terry handed the unfinished note Bob had written to Mrs. Vetter, who carried it over to a table lamp to read it.

Uncle Joe walked over to Aaron with his hand out-stretched. "Thank you, young man, for being in the right place at the right time." He smiled.

"Who is this young man?" asked Aunt Marie.

Fern took hold of Aaron's hand and looked her mother in the eye. "Mom and Dad, this is Aaron."

Aaron pushed his glasses up on his nose and smiled sheepishly. "Aaron, these are my parents," Fern told him.

"How long have you two known each other?" asked Aunt Marie.

Fern smiled. "Quite awhile."

"Yes, ma'am," Aaron answered, his head lowered.

"Aaron has been staying in one of the cottages across the lake," explained Fern.

"I see," said Uncle Joe. He sighed, looking the young man

over with a frown. "Well, young man, it looks like you could use a shower."

Everybody laughed, and then Aaron stuck his hands in his pockets and stared at the floor. "I wouldn't mind that," he said, "but then I'll leave."

"You don't have a shower in your house?" asked Mrs. Vetter.

Fern was afraid he would reveal too much, so she ushered Aaron into the hallway toward the main bathroom. "I'll get you some towels," she told him.

Uncle Joe shrugged and walked over to the fireplace to add some logs.

"I'd better go check on Ruby," said Mrs. Vetter as she gave the note back to Terry. She started upstairs, but then turned to Annette and Penny and said, "There's some supper waiting for you in the kitchen."

"We're gonna clean up first," said Annette and beckoned to Penny to follow her.

"So much has happened," Penny said as they headed for the girls' bathroom upstairs. "And Ruby's really scared that she won't see her dad again. Annette, what are we gonna do?"

"I don't know, Pen, but I don't have a good feeling about Bob."

"He saved your life," Penny reminded her.

"And I think he's breaking Ruby's heart," Annette said bitterly. As they passed their room on the way to the bathroom, they could hear Ruby sobbing and Mrs. Vetter trying to console the girl. Penny sighed and shook her head.

An hour later, even though it was after ten o'clock, the family gathered in the dining room as Aunt Marie and Mrs. Vetter laid out a buffet of ham and side dishes. The girls told about their ordeal during the storm when they'd had to steer the canoe to the nearest shore. Fern told her parents how they had made their way through the woods to the deserted cabin, and how they had discovered it was a storehouse for goods stolen by the three thieves.

"How did you happen to show up?" Annette asked Aaron, who was seated beside Fern and was eating food like it was going out of style. He chewed, then swallowed and wiped his mouth with a napkin.

"I was out on a walk after you left my cabin," he told them. "The storm was coming up, but I happened to notice that somebody was sneaking around one of the cabins nearby. It was Darrell and his friends. I hid, then followed them through the woods as they carried big bags of stuff out of somebody's cottage and took it over to the cabin you girls went into. They must have just left it when you four showed up."

"The light we saw must have been from them," surmised Penny.

"Anyway," Aaron continued, "I watched and I saw them leave. They returned to the house they'd just robbed and got more stuff. That's when the bear came into the picture, and Fern and you, Penny … took off running."

"The bear attacked them," Penny remembered. "We could hear their screams as we ran back to the cabin."

"We had no idea you were nearby," Fern said to Aaron.

"Brenda had that .22 rifle," Aaron said. "She thought it would stop a bear." He rolled his eyes. "It only stunned him, but it wasn't long before that bear charged again."

Uncle Joe, with his arms folded on the table, studied Aaron. "Where are you from, young man?"

Fern started to fidget as Aaron cleared his throat, then said, "I'm from Oshkosh."

"You got a job?"

"No, sir." Aaron stared in his lap, then looked up at Fern's father and stated, "I'm actually on my way to Canada, sir."

"My goodness," mumbled Aunt Marie as she exchanged

glances with Mrs. Vetter.

"Why Canada?" Uncle Joe's deep brown eyes pierced Aaron's.

"I want to look for work there," Aaron explained.

Ruby spoke up for the first time since they'd sat down to eat. "He's a draft dodger, Uncle Joe."

There was silence. Annette noticed Uncle Joe did not take his eyes off the boy, who just sat there staring down at his plate. Fern's brown eyes were darting left and right and she didn't know how to react.

Terry was the one who put down his fork and stood up, pushing his chair away from the table. "Unbelievable," he muttered, picking up his plate to carry into the kitchen.

Ruby sniffled. "My dad is a hero," she told the others. "He fought in Vietnam. He's been in the Air Force a long, long time." She looked over at Aaron and said with squinty eyes, "You are afraid. You won't go in the Army because you're a coward."

Aaron didn't know what to say. He sniffed, wiped his mouth and pushed his chair back from the table. "I think I'll go now," he said.

"Daddy," Fern pleaded, "please ... can't Aaron stay here at the lake house tonight? He's been through an ordeal."

"No, Fern," argued Aaron. "I think it's best I go."

She stood up. "No, Aaron."

"Joe," said Aunt Marie, reaching over and placing her hand on her husband's arm, "the boy helped capture the thieves. We have room and certainly we can accommodate him for one night."

The tension in the room was overwhelming. Nobody moved. After half a minute, Uncle Joe let out a deep sigh and Annette noticed a quiver in his jaw line. Then he slowly got up from the table and walked out of the dining room.

Aaron turned to Aunt Marie and said humbly, "Thank

you for the meal, ma'am. I'm sorry that I caused a problem."

"You can't go, Aaron!" cried Fern, beside herself. "Mama …
please go talk to Daddy."

"No, Fern," said Aaron, smiling at her. "It's all right."

"But …" Fern was close to tears.

Terry came in from the kitchen after dumping his dishes.
He called to Aaron, "Hey, man, I'll drive you around the lake."
He looked at Mrs. Vetter, who nodded consent, and then the
two of them left the lake house.

After the meal, Annette and Penny helped clear the table.
Fern had run up to her room, humiliated and upset. Ruby had
retired to the living room, where she spread herself out on the
rug in front of the fireplace, petting Jabbo, who was content to
lie there and soak up the heat.

"We'll take care of the dishes," Mrs. Vetter told Annette.
"You girls should get ready for bed."

Dismissed, Annette and Penny dragged their tired bodies
upstairs to their room. They got into their nightgowns, then sat
on the bed and talked over all that had happened that day.

"It's not fair of Uncle Joe not to let Aaron stay the night,"
said Penny. "Poor Fern."

"I don't know what to think about it," Annette confessed.
"On one hand, Aaron is a draft dodger and he's wanted for not
showing up for service. On the other hand, he seems like a
really nice person. And Fern really cares about him."

"Yeah, that's the hard part," said Penny. "She might try to
run away with him."

"I hope not," said Annette. "That would be a huge
mistake."

The door opened slowly and Ruby entered the room.

"Hi, Ruby," said Annette. "Are you tired?"

The girl nodded her head and went to her suitcase to get
out her pajamas.

"We're sorry your dad left," said Penny. "But maybe he'll

be back."

"Yeah," added Annette, but she could tell her sister didn't buy it.

"This has been the worst spring break I've ever had," Ruby said at last. "I just want to go back to Ravensville. I'm going to go back with Mom and Terry when they leave tomorrow."

"They're leaving?" asked Penny.

"Yes," said Annette. "I heard Mom say they'd be driving back first thing in the morning."

"I think you should stay with *us*, Ruby," said Penny.

"Why?" The girl's eyes were filled with hurt. "I'm not having a good time. I want to go home."

Annette collapsed upon the bed she shared with Penny, and after Ruby climbed into the other bed that she would share with their mother, Penny turned off the light and the room was dark. They listened to Ruby's sniffles until they couldn't stay awake any longer.

21

An Upsetting Morning

It was eleven-thirty at night when Bob pulled his Ford Falcon into the campsite beside the lake. Not more than twenty minutes had passed since Terry had driven past it on his way back to the lake house after taking Aaron home to his hut. Bob was drained and needed sleep.

After the deputies had arrested the two fugitives at the cabin, Bob had limped back to his car. His leg had grown painful after he and Joe Parker had chased after the two delinquents.

But when he'd arrived at his parked car after leaving the cabin, nobody was around. He had half expected Ruby and the girls to be there, waiting for him. Apparently someone else had already given them a ride—and Joe as well.

Bob had no idea where the Parkers' lake house was. He only knew that it was somewhere on the other side of the lake. But there were a lot of lodges across the lake, and he wasn't sure he'd have been welcome to stay at the lake house as it was.

He did remember, though, how elated Ruby had been to see him. At the time, he'd just felt overwhelmed with every-thing that was happening. He was in pain, so he had jumped in his car and driven to town to see if the convenience store was still open. He needed to get some aspirin.

His head was full of what he called "helmet fire," and the stressful situation with the bear and the fugitive youths had brought up some ugly memories from Vietnam. He certainly had not wanted anyone—especially Ruby—to see him in that frame of mind.

The stars were visible in a clear sky above Lake Minocqua as Bob slowly climbed out from behind the wheel to pick up his things he had left beside the campfire, which was now extinguished and cold. That's when he noticed his camouflage backpack was missing, along with his thermos of coffee and whatever else he had left on the ground before he heard the gunshots. He had grabbed his Ruger and run off in the direction of the firing.

For a minute or two, Bob puzzled over the missing items. Finally, he sighed and turned back to his car. He was too tired to think. He almost wished he had just gotten a motel room again in town. But he'd needed to buy aspirin. He had very little money left and there was no sense using up the little bit of gas left in his tank.

Early the next morning, Annette awoke next to Penny in the double bed. Ruby was still sound asleep in the other bed, but Mrs. Vetter had already gotten up and was probably already downstairs.

It had not been a good night for Annette. She had tossed and turned, disturbed by the events that had occurred since their adventure in the storm with the canoe, followed by their chilly trek through the woods to the cabin. The bear attack was still vivid in her mind, and her brain reeled from all the activity.

More than anything, however, she felt badly for Ruby and Terry. Why had Bob Foley taken off? Why had he written that note? How could he just disappear when he'd traveled all this way to find his kids? Something nagged at her as she tiptoed to her suitcase so as not to wake the other girls. She just could not believe Ruby's father would run away, unless …

Gazing at herself in the mirror of the dresser, her auburn hair was all mussed up from tossing and turning half the night. Unless … maybe Bob had something to hide. Maybe there was more to his story than any of them knew. With a sigh, she picked out her clothes, then noiselessly got dressed.

Mrs. Vetter was downstairs in the kitchen, talking to Aunt Marie and Uncle Joe, who were sitting around drinking coffee. They all looked very concerned. "Good morning, Annette," said Aunt Marie when she walked in.

"Morning." Annette stifled a yawn and joined them at the table.

"You look like you didn't get much sleep," remarked Mrs. Vetter. "Well, neither did I." She sipped her coffee.

"Would you like some toast and some juice, Annette?" asked her aunt.

"Not right now," said Annette. "Ruby and Penny are still sleeping."

"That poor angel," crooned Aunt Marie.

"Terry's outside checking the oil in the car," Annette's mother told her. "We're heading back to Ravensville soon."

"Are you taking Ruby with you?" Annette asked anxiously, remembering what the girl had said last night.

"No, I think she needs to stay here," said Mrs. Vetter. "She's upset, but it won't do her any good coming back to Ravensville."

Uncle Joe picked up his mug and walked out of the kitchen. "I'll tell Fern you're leaving," he said to Mrs. Vetter.

"Poor Fern," said Aunt Marie after her husband left the room. She shook her head.

"Aaron seems like such a nice boy," commented Mrs. Vetter.

"Joe told me how helpful he was last night," added Aunt

Marie.

When Terry came in from outside, he went to the sink to wash his hands. "Morning, Annette."

"Hi, Terry," she said. Then she asked him, "Was Bob's car still gone when you took Aaron home last night?"

"Yup," said Terry. "I'm afraid he won't be back."

"I just don't understand it," said Annette. "What do you suppose is wrong?"

"Marie!" Uncle Joe shouted from the hallway. The big dark-complected man strutted into the kitchen, his face full of concern. "Fern's gone."

"What?" Aunt Marie wrinkled up her face.

"She's not in her bedroom, and I think she didn't sleep in her bed last night."

Both Aunt Marie and Mrs. Vetter stood up from the table. The two women followed Uncle Joe back out while Annette stared at Terry, who wiped his hands with a towel and poured himself a cup of coffee.

"Sounds like trouble," said Annette.

"She probably split," said Terry, bringing his coffee to the table. "She was angry with her dad over Aaron."

"Do you think she ran away with him?"

Terry shrugged and reached for the cream and sugar. A minute later, the three adults returned to the kitchen, all frantic with worry.

"Fern left a note on her dresser," said Aunt Marie. "She said she's going to Canada … with Aaron!" Suddenly, she burst into tears.

"Well, I'll put a stop to that!" Uncle Joe thundered as he stormed out of the room.

"What are you going to do, Joe?" Mrs. Vetter called after him, then came over to comfort her sister.

"What's going on?" Penny popped into the room, all wide-eyed. "What happened?"

Annette quickly explained the situation, then asked, "Is Ruby still asleep?"

"No, she's up," said Penny. "She wanted to take a shower."

"I guess this means our trip home will be delayed," Mrs. Vetter said to Terry.

"Okay with me," he said. "But maybe someone should give Tim a call … let him know what's up."

"Can I call him?" Annette volunteered.

Mrs. Vetter was still comforting Aunt Marie, who had understood their concern even in her upset over Fern's absence. She waved at Annette to go ahead and make the call.

Penny stayed in the kitchen with Terry as Annette made her way through the dining room into the lobby. Uncle Joe had left the lake house and she heard his car starting up in the driveway. Annette found the telephone and dialed the Duncans' phone number direct long distance.

After about five rings, Audrey Duncan answered. "Hello?"

"Mrs. Duncan," said Annette.

"Why, Annette. Are you home?"

"No, I'm in Minocqua."

"Oh. Well, is everything all right?"

"Uh … yes, kind of," said Annette. "Can I please speak to Tim?"

"He just came in from the barn," said Mrs. Duncan. "Tim … it's Annette …"

A moment later, Tim's voice met her ears. "Hello, Annette." His warm voice lit up her heart and she started coiling the telephone cord around her finger.

"Tim, I thought I should give you a call and let you know that Terry may not be back today. I know he was supposed to work over at the Randts' and also help you out."

"Why? Are you all right? What happened?" Tim's tone changed to one of concern.

"Oh, it would take too long to explain it all." Annette sighed, but her voice was cracking with emotion. "I almost got eaten by a ... a *bear*."

"What!"

Then she giggled. "And that's not all. Oh ... I don't want to take up time telling you everything that happened."

Tim hesitated, then asked, "Did Ruby's and Terry's dad show up?"

"Actually, yes," said Annette, "but that's another thing ... he disappeared on us. Ruby is very upset, and so is Terry."

"Gad," said Tim. "I'm sorry to hear that. What else?"

"My cousin has run away," said Annette.

"Well, this is starting to sound like a soap opera," said Tim. Just as he spoke, Annette saw Uncle Joe come in through the front door.

"Fern's boyfriend is ... well, Tim, I can't talk now."

"I see," he said. "Well, any idea when Terry and your mom will be coming back?"

"Maybe as early as tonight," Annette disclosed. "I guess it depends on what happens next around here. What a spring break this has been."

"I wish I were there," said Tim.

There was a pause and then Annette said, "Me too, Tim. It's good to hear your voice."

"I've missed you," he said.

Annette's heart quickened and she smiled. "I can't wait to get home."

"If I know you, there's a mystery involved," Tim said. "Annette, promise me that you'll be careful. Will you promise me?"

"Oh, Tim ..."

"Annette ... don't make me drive up there." He was smiling, she could tell.

"Okay, I promise. I'll be careful."

Mrs. Vetter walked in just then and signaled to Annette. "Uncle Joe needs to use the phone."

"I've gotta go, Tim."

"Okay. Bye."

"Bye, Tim." She hung up with a smile on her face, even with the lake house in an uproar.

22

A Change of Heart

Bob awoke Tuesday morning from the sound of traffic. Sitting up in the back seat of his Falcon, he noticed two county sheriff cars driving up the road that went to vacation cabins on the lake. Apparently a crew had been sent to retrieve the stolen goods that Darrell, Brenda and Nick had taken from various cottages on the lake. All of the past night's events flooded his mind as he shrugged off his blankets and sat up in the back seat of the car.

It was a clear, pretty April morning, and the sun was shining through the trees. He could see the glimmer of sunlight on the lake out his windshield. Exhaustion had resulted in deep sleep for him, which had been badly needed. He decided that today he was going to find the lake house and his kids. He now regretted the fact that he had driven off on an impulse without waiting to find out where he could meet Terry and Ruby later.

Without his knapsack, he couldn't make a cup of coffee, but he got a fire going anyway. If for nothing else, sitting and watching the flames as they warmed him would help him think and come up with a plan. The Falcon needed more gasoline and he had very little money. However, he had gone without food for days in the jungles of Vietnam, under worse conditions than he found himself in now.

The hunger didn't bother him. The possibility that he'd lost his chance to be with his kids did. He also took notice that no one had come back to his campsite … at least not that he knew of … so perhaps he had been right, and they didn't want him there.

And if that was the case, what now? What was he to do? He had nowhere to go. No home, no family … he was just a forgotten war veteran with issues … and not wanting to be a burden to anybody.

Yet he still recalled the look on his little girl's face when she had recognized him. He could not forget that. He owed it to the kids to see them one last time and to say goodbye. He wanted them to be happy and in a family that was stable.

The farmhouse in Ravensville where he had stopped seemed very quaint and inviting. Even the collie that had greeted him made him smile, and the tall neighbor boy had been kind and friendly toward him.

After washing his face in the lake, Bob put out the campfire and got back into his car. He wasn't sure he could make it to town on empty, but he had to try. He dug out his car key and plugged it into the ignition. He was relieved when the engine turned over.

"Fern, what are you doing here?" Aaron stood at the door of his shack. He had heard someone banging on the door and had been roused from sleep. He hadn't expected to find Fern standing out in the cold. He immediately invited her inside.

"Oh, Aaron." She had been crying and her eyes were red as she stepped inside his hovel. "I'm so embarrassed by what my dad said to you last night."

"Don't give it a second thought," said Aaron. He held her as she pushed her way into his arms. "But that doesn't answer my question. Why are you here?"

"I'm not going back," she said, her lip trembling as her dark brown eyes looked into his. "I'm running away. I want to go to Canada … with you."

"Are you nuts?" Aaron backed away and looked at her, astonished. "Why would you want to do that?"

"Because I want to be with you," said Fern.

The tall boy with scraggly hair rubbed his mouth as he paced nervously in front of the door. "Fern … you can't."

"Why not? Aaron, what's wrong? Don't you want to be with me?"

"Fern, I won't let you do that. You have a mom and a dad who love you. Please don't do something you'll regret later. You don't know how good you have it living at the lake house."

Fern was struggling not to cry, but tears were seeping out against her will. Her lower lip jutted out as she thought about what he had said. "Are you really going all the way to Canada?" she asked him.

Aaron sighed and stuck his hands in his jeans pockets. "Eventually … yes. I had planned on sticking it out here as long as I could."

"But the authorities know about you now," Fern argued. "They'll send someone after you now that they know you're here."

"I know," he said.

"So maybe it's time to go," she said. "I have a little money I had saved in a jar." She reached into her pocket, but Aaron reached out and stopped her.

"I don't want your money, Fern."

"But … we can start a new life up in Canada," Fern said hopefully. "It'll be groovy."

"Fern … think about what you are saying."

"I *have* thought about it. I laid awake most the night."

Aaron only sighed.

"There are plenty of others like us," Fern tried to convince him. "You know, kids opposed to the war. I'll bet there's a whole community up in Canada. We can be part of the resistance."

"Listen to you!" Aaron turned on her, angry now. "You're beginning to sound like that Darrell and Brenda ... and ... and poor Nick."

Devastated, Fern turned away from him and began sobbing. She sank to her knees on the rotten floorboards and cried.

Aaron walked over to her and put his hands on her shoulders. "I won't lower myself to the likes of them," he told Fern. "Actually, I've been giving it a lot of thought. I don't feel good about myself anymore, and I'm thinking I'll turn myself in and ... and join up." He choked a little on the last two words.

Fern cried even louder now and forced herself to her feet. "Aaron, no! Why? Why would you do that?"

"It's not too late," he said, trying to reason with her. "I made a mistake. Doesn't everybody make mistakes now and then?"

"But ... yes, but ..."

"I don't like fighting," Aaron said, looking Fern in the eye. "I hate wars. I admit, the idea of going to Vietnam freaks me out. But then I think of all the guys who had to go. I met one of them last night ... that Bob guy."

"He's Ruby's father," Fern explained.

Aaron nodded. "Yes, I know. But what I'm saying is, he made an impression on me, Fern. He was actually over there. He was captured and he escaped ... and he made it back. How do you think that makes me feel? Like a low-life, that's what ... no wonder your dad acted the way he did toward me. Who could blame him?"

Fern wiped her eyes. "My brother David is over there

now. We worry about him. We wonder every day, is he coming home?"

"That's what I'm talking about," said Aaron. "If you go to Canada with me, your parents will have no one. They won't have David and they won't have you. How is that going to make them feel? Do you really want to live with that on your conscience?"

"But I care about you," she insisted.

"You hardly know me," said Aaron.

Suddenly, there was a knock on the door. Both kids jumped and stared at each other—fearful. Then Fern sauntered off into a corner while Aaron slowly made his way to the door. He peeked out the cracked window and then slowly turned the knob.

Ruby had come out of the shower and was slowly and methodically brushing out her long blond hair in their guest room when Annette came in to check on her. "Everyone's having breakfast downstairs," she told her sister. "Are you hungry?"

Ruby appeared lethargic and mumbled, "No."

"You need to eat something," insisted Annette, sitting down on the bed. "I know you're upset about your dad. But Terry and Mom decided to stay at the lake house today. They want to help you find him."

For a moment, there was a glimmer of hope on Ruby's sad face, but then she turned away. "How can they do that?" she asked. "Nobody knows where he is. Besides, maybe he doesn't want us to find him."

"But, Ruby, he drove all the way from Colorado Springs. When Tim told him we were here in Minocqua, he drove all the way up north … and he finally found you last night."

"Then why did he write that letter, and why did he leave?" Ruby set the brush down and glared at Annette.

"While you were in the shower," said Annette in order to change the subject, "Uncle Joe discovered that Fern ran away."

"She did?" Ruby's blue eyes widened.

"She left a note saying she was running away to Canada with Aaron."

"Oh, Annette …" Ruby stood up. "Poor Fern …"

"*No* … poor Aunt Marie and Uncle Joe," said Annette.

"Maybe they can stop her in time," said Ruby. "I'll go downstairs with you. Maybe we can help find Fern for them."

Annette smiled and gave Ruby a hug. "It's going to turn out all right, Ruby."

The girl sighed but said nothing, and then the two of them went downstairs to join the others.

Fern looked up as Aaron let Bob Foley into the dwelling. Bob looked around at the lack of furnishings, then said, "So this is where you live?"

"Yeah," said Aaron. "Bob … we were just discussing you."

Fern turned to face him and smiled. "Hello."

Bob nodded, then faced Aaron and said, "My car ran out of gas. I need a ride to town."

"Well, I don't have a car," said Aaron apologetically.

"Oh," said Bob, stroking his mustache. He kept looking over at Fern, then at Aaron.

"I walked over from the lake house," Fern told Bob. "It takes about an hour to get around the lake."

Bob frowned and Aaron quickly told Fern, "Bob's got a bum leg."

"Why don't you take the canoe?" suggested Fern.

"Oh yeah," said Aaron. "The canoe is still over by the swamp, isn't it?"

"I hope so," said Fern.

Aaron explained to Bob how the girls had gotten caught

in yesterday's storm and had been forced to reach shore, which is how they had ended up at the deserted cabin with all the loot from the trio of thieves.

"But I don't know where the lake house is," Bob confessed sheepishly.

Aaron and Fern looked at each other. She dropped her head and sighed. "I guess you win, Aaron. Let's get the canoe and take Bob across the lake."

"But I don't want to disturb anyone," Bob said in protest.

Fern stuck her hands on her hips. "Are you kidding me? Ruby is devastated. She believes you have deserted her. They found the letter you wrote."

Bob held his head and shook it slowly side to side. "Oh, no ... that was my diary." He looked up at the two of them. "I'm in the habit of writing down my thoughts in letter form. It helps me sort things out. That wasn't a letter to the kids. You mean they thought ..."

"Come on," said Fern. "Aaron, you come too. Let's take Bob to the lake house."

"Thanks, you two." Bob managed a smile.

Aaron put his arm around Fern's shoulder and then ushered the two of them out of his shack into the morning sunshine. "It's not too far to the swamp," he reassured Bob, who was walking with a worse limp after his trek that morning from his campsite.

"Maybe half a mile," said Fern. "Think you can make it?"

"I can make it," Bob muttered, remembering the jungle.

"Here, take my walking stick." Aaron turned around and grabbed his long hickory stick from near the doorway. He handed it to Bob, who nodded in gratitude. Then the three of them started out for the swamp.

23

The Return

A fter breakfast, Uncle Joe decided to go into town and submit a report on his missing daughter at the police station. The girls volunteered to wash up the breakfast dishes while Mrs. Vetter consoled Aunt Marie.

Terry went outside to walk around in the backyard and decide a course of action toward looking for his stepfather. He just could not believe that Bob would pull something like that —just take off and disappoint Ruby the way he had. Didn't he know how fragile the girl was since Colorado Springs, and all of the trauma surrounding their mother's suicide?

Well, obviously not. Maybe something had happened to him in Vietnam. Ruby had mentioned he had a scar on his face and walked with a limp. But it didn't make sense for the man to just desert them after he'd traveled so far to see them.

He was also worried about his two employers in Ravensville. He had planned to work through spring break and earn a little money. He knew the Duncans might be having more trouble with their milking machine, but most of all he had looked forward to helping Mr. Randt and his sons fix the pasture fences on their farm. The Randts were poor and really needed his help. It wasn't so much the money as it was the desire to help them out. He hated to waste another day here at the lake house, yet they needed to stay another day after all that occurred.

A station wagon pulled into the parking lot of the lake house while Terry was walking back toward the front. As he got closer, a middle-aged man and woman got out of the car. He didn't recognize them as the Snyders until he was closer and they greeted him.

"We brought something," said Roger as he pulled an object out of the back seat. Terry came closer and saw that it was a .22 rifle. "We found this in the woods this morning when Myrtle and I were on our morning walk."

"Where in the woods?" asked Terry. He hadn't been a witness to the bear shooting.

"Not too far from that cabin where the bear was killed," said Myrtle. "We figured maybe the gun belongs to one of you."

Just then, Aunt Marie stepped out the front door, followed by Annette, Penny and Ruby. "Well, hello," she called out to the couple. "Roger? Myrtle? What brings you by?"

Annette smiled at the neighborly couple, once again grateful how they had given them a ride home last night.

"We missed the chapel service on Easter morning," Myrtle said apologetically, "but we heard that one of the girls staying with you did a superb job with the music."

"Yes, we're sorry we missed that now," said Roger, looking around at the girls. "Which one was it?"

Aunt Marie put her hand on Penny's arm. "This one is the talented one," she said with a smile. "Penny is a friend of my niece, Annette, who came up for the week from Ravensville."

"Where's Ravensville?" asked Myrtle.

Before she could answer, Annette noticed the .22 rifle and Roger held it up for them to see. "This belong to any of you?"

"That's the rifle Annette tried to kill the bear with," said Ruby, "but it wasn't loaded."

"Oh, my goodness!" exclaimed Aunt Marie.

"But my dad shot the bear," Ruby affirmed. "If he hadn't, Annette might not be here today."

"Let me see." Terry reached out and Roger Snyder let him take the rifle. He then slid open the bolt, which revealed the chamber was empty.

"The thieves got that rifle from the man who drowned," Annette related. "We heard them bragging about it."

"Leroy?" Aunt Marie looked shocked.

"Terrible shame about poor Leroy," said Myrtle. "He was a regular at your lake house, wasn't he?"

"Yes," said Aunt Marie. "We'll miss him."

"Did they say what he died from?" asked Roger.

"He had a bad heart," said Aunt Marie.

"Well, it wouldn't surprise me if those kids had something to do with it," the man added.

"Maybe we should let the police know about the gun," suggested Annette.

"Good idea," said Aunt Marie. "Joe went to police headquarters this morning." She didn't tell them about Fern leaving the note.

"Where's Mom?" Terry asked, noticing that Mrs. Vetter wasn't present.

"Oh, she wanted to call the hospital," said Aunt Marie.

When Myrtle looked alarmed, Penny piped in, "She had to call in and say she's taking another day off. Annette's mom is a nurse."

"Oh." Myrtle smiled in relief.

"Has anyone heard anything about those varmints?" asked Roger.

"You mean those kids?" asked Aunt Marie. "No. Maybe Joe will know something when he gets back."

They chatted a little longer, and then the Snyders said they had to leave, that they had some errands to run in town. Aunt Marie thanked them for stopping by, and then the neighbors from across the lake left and everyone returned to the house.

Mrs. Vetter was just hanging up the phone.

"Everything settled?" asked Aunt Marie.

"For now," said Mrs. Vetter. "But they're missing me."

"Well, of course."

Terry closed up the rifle and handed it to Aunt Marie, who went behind the counter of the registration desk and propped it against the wall. "It's not loaded," Terry told her.

"When are we gonna start looking for my dad?" asked Ruby.

"Right now," said Terry.

"That's why Terry and I decided to stay," Mrs. Vetter told her. "Ruby, before I called the hospital, I got hold of Uncle Will. I called him at work and he happened to be in the office, so I told him about your dad. He's going to make some phone calls."

"But how are we gonna find him?" Ruby blinked her eyes, quite worried.

"Well, first," said Terry, "we're gonna drive around the area and look for him."

"Can we go now?" asked Ruby.

"I don't see why not," said Mrs. Vetter.

Just then, Uncle Joe came through the front door. "Guess what?" he said as they all gathered around him. "I talked to one of the deputies down at the cop shop, and the girl confessed to their operation. Apparently, she turned against that Darrell boy, accusing him of killing the red-headed one. Can't remember his name …"

"Nick," said Penny. "What did she say?"

Uncle Joe put his car keys on the counter and continued.

"It turns out the kid ... the red-headed punk ... was planning to rat on the two older ones. They got in some argument yesterday. Nick wanted to leave while the getting was good, but the other two insisted on staying and causing more trouble. Then ... she threatened him with that .22 rifle they had. Said she used that rifle to shoot the bear when it was attacking Darrell, her boyfriend ... but Aaron showed up. Aaron told them a .22 wouldn't kill a bear, and that because the bear was wounded, it would charge them. She said he was right."

"What was Aaron doing there with them?" asked Aunt Marie.

Annette spoke up. "He had been watching them," she explained. "He said he'd followed them and found out where they were hiding the stuff they stole, which was at the cabin we went to after we beached the canoe in the storm."

"Aaron was going to finger them?" asked Uncle Joe.

"Yes," said Terry. "And that's why he was there when the bear attacked and killed Nick, after the bear caused the deputy's car to crash."

"What a brave thing to do," said Aunt Marie.

"And that .22 happens to be right over here," said Terry, walking to the corner behind the counter and picking up the rifle. He handed it to Uncle Joe.

"That's Leroy's gun," said Uncle Joe, examining it carefully.

"Yes," said Annette, "that's what we heard those kids say. They got it from Leroy."

"If there was a struggle, maybe those kids caused Leroy's death," said Mrs. Vetter.

"I'm calling the station," said Uncle Joe and headed for the telephone.

Ruby sighed and walked toward the front door. "When are we gonna go look for my dad?" she asked.

"In a while," Annette assured her as her attention focused

on Uncle Joe making the call. She didn't notice Ruby slip outside, and nobody gave it a thought as the girl disappeared around the side of the lake house and headed toward the pier.

"Nobody listens to me," Ruby whimpered as she wandered closer to the lakeshore and stepped onto the pier. "Nobody cares ..." Then she sat down and dangled her legs close to the water. There was a slight breeze, but the day was already starting to warm up. So far, it was the warmest day of spring break.

"My dad ..." Ruby murmured and immediately thought about the words to her favorite song called *My Dad*. She began to hum the tune and then sang, *"My dad ... now here is a man he is everything strong ... no, he can't do wrong ... my dad ..."** Then she let herself cry. She buried her face in her arms and just let the tears come.

She thought of her younger days, when her father had been a big part of her life. Yes, he had been strict. He had been somewhat of a disciplinarian, yet she hadn't minded. Living on Air Force bases, her close friends had said the same thing about their parents who were in the military.

Her fondest memories of him had been walks in the park, the State Fair one year, helping her with homework, surprising her one day with a goldfish in a bowl, and many instances where the two of them had become close and shared stories, songs and plans for the future.

Then, in the last three or four years, her father had been involved with his work more and more, and he was absent from home for long stretches, before being deployed overseas about a year ago. That had been the hardest time of all, not only for Ruby and Terry, but especially for their mother, Ruth, who had really grown worse with her drinking.

"Dad ... come home," Ruby sobbed. "I miss you. I'm glad you're alive ... but I don't want you to go away again." She

* *My Dad*, lyrics by Paul Petersen

broke into a new series of sobs.

"Where's Ruby?" Annette asked when she realized she hadn't seen her sister in a while. Nobody knew, nor had anyone seen Ruby slip outside.

"I'll check up in our room." Penny hurried upstairs.

Aunt Marie looked in the kitchen. Uncle Joe was still on the phone, and Mrs. Vetter checked the downstairs bathroom and hallway. "No sign of her," she reported.

Terry and Annette went out the back door and saw the blonde girl sitting on the end of the pier, dangling her feet over the water. In the distance, they could make out a craft on the lake with three people in it.

"Terry, she's been crying," said Annette.

"Come on," he beckoned, and the two of them walked quickly toward the pier.

As they reached the dock, Annette shielded her eyes and saw that the craft was a canoe and that it was heading toward them.

"Ruby!" Terry called out.

The girl looked up at him, but didn't move.

"Terry," said Annette, pointing out into the lake. "Look, it's the canoe."

Terry stood beside her and shielded his eyes from the sun. "You're right. Who's that in it? Wait. Is that Fern?"

The people in the canoe were looking at them. The dark-haired tall girl paddling was definitely Fern, Annette decided. She waved and called out, "Fern!"

"I think that's Aaron with her," said Terry.

Ruby suddenly noticed the approaching canoe and stood up at the end of the pier. Aaron was paddling on the other side of the canoe, and the man sitting in front of them tried to stand up in the canoe, but Fern pulled him back down and the canoe rocked a bit.

"I don't believe it," said Terry. "Can it be?"

"Oh, my gosh," breathed Annette.

"It's him," added Terry.

Ruby suddenly let out a squeal and began waving wildly toward the canoe. "Dad!" she shouted. "Dad! Oh, Dad!"

"Be careful, Ruby." Afraid that the girl was going to fall into the water, Annette ran out onto the pier and managed to grab Ruby before she slipped off the pier.

Fern steered the canoe toward them. She was smiling and so was Aaron. Bob Foley was focused on his daughter's face, and as soon as the canoe pulled up against the pier, Fern and Aaron held it fast while Terry stepped forth and reached out his hand to Bob.

"Hello, son," Bob said with a warm smile.

"Daddy!" Ruby shrieked.

Bob staggered a bit as he stepped onto the pier. "Ruby!" he called, then embraced his daughter. The two of them wept while Terry helped Fern and Aaron get out of the canoe and together they pulled it alongside the pier and tied it.

"My dad is back! My dad is back!" Ruby shouted as they all headed for the lake house.

"Terry ..." Bob broke away from Ruby a moment to give his stepson a bear hug.

"Bob ... Dad, I mean ... welcome home." Terry laughed.

Someone shouted from the lake house, and a moment later the rest of them came running to greet the new arrivals. Penny's green eyes were wide and Aunt Marie embraced Fern while Uncle Joe rushed over to Aaron and shook his hand.

"I apologize for what I said last night, young man," said Uncle Joe. "I was wrong about you."

"No need to apologize, sir. I couldn't let Fern leave her family," said Aaron.

"I'm sorry, Daddy," said Fern. "And Mama, will you forgive me?" She gave her mother a hug, then said, "I love you both so much."

Mrs. Vetter stood, staring at Ruby's father, and suddenly Bob caught her gaze and stared back. "*You* ..." Mrs. Vetter finally spoke. "Why, you ... you're the man I saw at the filling station in Tomahawk."

Both Terry and Annette looked at one another and shrugged.

"I don't believe I've had the pleasure." Bob reached out his hand, smiling from ear to ear.

Annette introduced them. "Mom, this is Bob Foley. Bob, this my mom, Helen Vetter."

"You're the lovely mother of these kids?" Bob took a step closer, but stumbled a bit. Mrs. Vetter immediately reached out and steadied him, then put her arm around him.

"Yes, I'm the proud mother of these three kids," she said, including Annette. "And I think we'd better get you to the lake house."

Ruby took hold of Bob's other hand, and everyone walked up to the lake house together. Fern and Aaron held hands while Fern explained to her father how Bob had run out of gas in his car, and how Aaron had changed his mind about being a draft dodger.

Penny took Annette aside and giggled. "Is this going to be a happy ending, or what?"

"What do you mean?" Annette asked, but she knew exactly what Penny was thinking. They both looked at Mrs. Vetter and Bob Foley, and how they had immediately started conversing and were smiling at one another as they reached the house.

"I believe this could be the beginning of something wonderful," Penny said with a sparkle in her eyes.

"Oh, Pen ... are you serious?" said Annette and then she giggled.

That afternoon, after a hearty lunch of chicken salad, fruit compote and brownies with ice cream—and after Bob had showered and was wearing a fresh set of clothes of Uncle Joe's—they relaxed. Everyone sat out on the back patio in lawn chairs and basked in the afternoon sun, staring at the lake. Ruby sat on one side of Bob, and Mrs. Vetter sat on the other.

Terry looked at Annette with a knowing glance, and she nodded in agreement. Fern and Aaron were sharing the porch swing while Penny chatted with Fern about school and her independent study next year with her music.

"Are you going back to Ravensville tomorrow with your mom and Bob?" Fern asked Annette later, after they'd had supper and the girls were cleaning up the kitchen. "Penny wants to go home. I guess she misses her boyfriend. Pete, isn't it?"

Annette smiled knowingly. "Yes, it's Pete. And yes, as much as I hate to cut spring break short, I think I've had enough excitement and need to rest before we go back to school next week. Plus poor Tim ... he's had to do double duty with milking our cow."

"You miss him, don't you?"

Annette blushed. "Absence makes the heart grow fonder," she muttered. Then she asked, "What's going to happen with Aaron?"

"He's going to stay here at the lake house for a few weeks," Fern said. "My father has some work for him to do before we get busy with the summer season. Then Aaron's going to apply for college, and he's going to sign up again for Selective Service."

"Oh Fern, that's good news." Then Annette asked, "But ... what if he gets drafted?"

"I'll deal with that when ... and *if* it happens."

"You've got the right attitude," said Penny, wiping a plate.

"What about Bob?" asked Fern.

"We're taking him home!" cried Ruby, who had just come into the kitchen and had overheard.

Everyone laughed, and then Ruby said, "I think Mom should marry my dad."

"*Shhh* ... somebody might hear you," warned Penny, glancing out the window.

"You said that about Uncle Will," Annette teased.

"Oh, I know," said Ruby, "but I think Mom's in love with my dad."

Annette messed up Ruby's hair and laughed. "Let's leave that up to Mom and Bob, shall we?"

"Ruby's certainly happy," commented Fern as the girl skipped out of the kitchen.

"I've never seen her happier," said Annette. She remembered the sound of Tim's voice on the phone earlier—how he had said, "*I miss you.*" There had been such feeling in his words that it dissolved any doubts she'd had about his commitment to her.

"Are you happy, Annette?" Penny asked, a gleam in her eye.

"More than you can know," Annette said with a smile as she hung the damp dish towel on the rack next to the sink. As much as she enjoyed being in Minocqua at the lake house, she secretly pined for the modest gray farmhouse outside Ravensville, her beloved collie, the woods ... and the dairy farmer's son who was longing for her to come home.

About the Author

Ann Carol Ulrich started writing the Annette Vetter series when she was 15, growing up in the '60s. She grew up in Monona, Wisconsin, but has lived in Michigan, Colorado, Ohio, Washington and Oregon. She currently is at home in Delta County, Colorado.

Visit her Author Website at **AnnUlrichMiller.com**, and Annette invites you to check her out on Facebook (*under the name Annette Vetter, of course*).

Spring Break at the Lake House (April 1969) is No. 7 in the Annette Vetter series.

Here are the earlier ones:

The Mystery at Hickory Hill (August 1968) takes place in the Cochetopa Hills of Colorado when Annette and Penny take a vacation out West before school starts.

The Secret of the Green Paint (September 1968) starts on the first day of school, when Annette makes a new friend in her Art class and also notices that new boy who lives on the farm down the road.

The Pouting Pumpkin Mystery (October 1968) celebrates Homecoming at Ravensville High, with a Halloween theme that involves HAM radio.

The Legend of the Lantern (November 1968) takes place over Thanksgiving weekend, during an early blizzard while Annette and Penny baby-sit for the Randt children while their mom has a new baby.

In the Shadow of the Tower (December 1968) introduces Terry and Ruby into the series, making Christmas a very special holiday for Annette, in addition to a new mystery.

The Ground Hog Mystery (February 1969) involves livestock rustlers in the county, following a hard Wisconsin winter. The Valentine's Dance is coming up, and Annette knows Pete is expecting her to ask him ... yet she longs to ask Tim Duncan instead. Ruby's nightmares are causing the Vetter family some concern, but stranger yet, Ruby's dreams have this weird connection to a missing pilot in Vietnam.

For more information on Annette Vetter books
and others in the Earth Star collection,
visit **www.earthstarpublications.com**

Spring Break at the Lake House
and all of the other *Annette Vetter Adventures*
are also available as eBooks at Amazon Kindle